CROSS KILL

Along Came a Spider killer Gary Soneji died years ago. But Alex Cross swears he sees Soneji gun down his partner. Is his greatest enemy back from the grave?

ZOO II

Humans are evolving into a savage new species that could save civilization—or end it. James Patterson's *Zoo* was just the beginning.

THE TRIAL

An accused killer will do anything to disrupt his own trial, including a courtroom shocker that Lindsay Boxer and the Women's Murder Club will never see coming.

LITTLE BLACK DRESS

Can a little black dress change everything? What begins as one woman's fantasy is about to go too far.

LET'S PLAY MAKE-BELIEVE

Christy and Marty just met, and it's love at first sight. Or is it? One of them is playing a dangerous game—and only one will survive.

LEARNING TO RIDE

City girl Madeline Harper never wanted to love a cowboy. But rodeo king Tanner Callen might change her mind…and win her heart.

THE McCULLAGH INN IN MAINE

Chelsea O'Kane escapes to Maine to build a new life—until she runs into Jeremy Holland, an old flame....

UPCOMING THRILLERS
BOOK**SHOTS**

113 MINUTES

Molly Rourke's son has been murdered. Now she'll do whatever it takes to get justice. No one should underestimate a mother's love....

HUNTED

Someone is luring men from the streets to play a mysterious, high-stakes game. Former Special Forces officer David Shelley goes undercover to shut it down—but will he win?

$10,000,000 MARRIAGE PROPOSAL

A mysterious billboard offering $10 million to get married intrigues three single women in LA. But who is Mr. Right...and is he the perfect match for the lucky winner?

FRENCH KISS

It's hard enough to move to a new city, but now everyone French detective Luc Moncrief cares about is being killed off. Welcome to New York.

KILLER CHEF

Caleb Rooney knows how to do two things: run a food truck and solve a murder. When people suddenly start dying of food-borne illnesses, the stakes are higher than ever....

THE CHRISTMAS MYSTERY

Two stolen paintings disappear from a Park Avenue murder scene—
French detective Luc Moncrief is in for a merry Christmas.

BLACK & BLUE

Detective Harry Blue is determined to take down the serial killer who's
abducted several women, but her mission leads to a shocking revelation.

UPCOMING ROMANCES

SACKING THE QUARTERBACK

Attorney Melissa St. James wins every case. Now, when she's up against
football superstar Grayson Knight, her heart is on the line too.

DAZZLING: THE DIAMOND TRILOGY, PART I

To support her artistic career, Siobhan Dempsey works at the elite
Stone Room in New York City…never expecting to be swept away by
Derick Miller.

THE MATING SEASON

Documentary ornithologist Sophie Castle is convinced that her heart
belongs only to the birds—until she meets her gorgeous cameraman,
Rigg Greensman.

BODYGUARD

Special Agent Abbie Whitmore has only one task: protect Congress-
man Jonathan Lassiter from a violent cartel's threats. Yet she's never had
to do it while falling in love.…

SOME GAMES AREN'T FOR CHILDREN....

After a nasty divorce, Christy Moore finds her escape in Marty Hawking, who introduces her to all sorts of experiences, including an explosive new game called "Make-Believe."

But what begins as innocent fun soon turns dark, and as Marty pushes the boundaries farther and farther, the game just may end up deadly.

Read the new jaw-dropping thriller *Let's Play Make-Believe,* available now from

BOOKSHOTS

CHASE

A MICHAEL BENNETT STORY

JAMES PATTERSON
MICHAEL LEDWIDGE

BOOK**SHOTS**

Little, Brown and Company

New York Boston London

Copyright © 2016 by James Patterson
Excerpt from *Hunted* copyright © 2016 by James Patterson

Hachette Book Group supports the right to free expression and the value of copyright. The purpose of copyright is to encourage writers and artists to produce the creative works that enrich our culture.

The scanning, uploading, and distribution of this book without permission is a theft of the author's intellectual property. If you would like permission to use material from the book (other than for review purposes), please contact permissions@hbgusa.com. Thank you for your support of the author's rights.

BookShots / Little, Brown and Company
Hachette Book Group
1290 Avenue of the Americas, New York, NY 10104
bookshots.com

First Edition: August 2016

BookShots is an imprint of Little, Brown and Company, a division of Hachette Book Group, Inc. The Little, Brown name and logo are trademarks of Hachette Book Group, Inc. The BookShots name and logo are trademarks of JBP Business, LLC.

The publisher is not responsible for websites (or their content) that are not owned by the publisher.

The Hachette Speakers Bureau provides a wide range of authors for speaking events. To find out more, go to hachettespeakersbureau.com or call (866) 376-6591.

ISBN 978-0-316-31717-7
LCCN 2016935247

10 9 8 7 6 5 4 3 2 1

RRD-C

Printed in the United States of America

PROLOGUE

FALL IN NEW YORK

ONE

AT THE END of the dark, crowded bar, a man in black twirled an e-cigarette through his fingers and over his thumb like a little baton, again and again as he watched and waited.

It was an aggravating, fidgety habit, he knew. But when he was anxious, it was harder to resist than smoking the damn thing.

The bar was in a hip industrial-chic hotel on 67th and Broadway called Index House, with a cutting-edge meets Roaring Twenties vibe. Charging stations blended into a décor of exposed brick and tufted chairs. With his downtown black silk suit and dark *GQ* looks, the man belonged there.

He deftly flipped the cigarette into his inside jacket pocket as the bartender finally approached with his drink. It was a Zombie, four or five different rums and some cognac with a splash of pineapple and mango juice. One of the rums was 151-proof, and flammable. He'd seen drinks lit on fire many times over the last seven years, in many places, from Jamaica to Jakarta.

Too damn many, he thought.

"So are you a *Walking Dead* fanatic, or do you just like the demon rum?" the doe-eyed bartender asked, over the crowd murmur and slow jazz piano playing from the lobby.

There were two bartenders, a guy and a girl, but he had ordered from the guy.

"Entschuldigen Sie?" he said, staring at her like he'd just stepped off a flying saucer. It meant "excuse me" in German. The one and only phrase he'd picked up in three useless months in Munich four years ago.

That did the trick. She went away with his two twenties, and quick. Lovely as she was, he didn't need any distractions. Not now. He began rubbing his thighs nervously as he scanned the hotel lobby. He looked out at the dark of Broadway through the plate glass behind him, a clear moonless October evening in New York, bright lights twinkling.

At this critical juncture, he needed to stay on his damn toes.

Where the hell is this guy? he thought, taking out his phone to check his messages. It was 9:25. Almost a half hour late and still no call. Did this joker's phone die? He just wasn't coming? No way to know. Great. He'd just sit here on his ass some more.

He placed his phone on the zinc bar top and reached for the drink. Then he stopped himself and instead took out the e-cigarette again. Back and forth, and back and forth, over and through his fingers faster and faster, he twirled the metal cigarette until it was just a black blur across his knuckles.

TWO

IN THE CROWDED library off the hotel bar, Devine sat listening to the boss man on the phone.

"What's Pretty Boy doing now?"

"Nothing," Devine said. "Just sitting at the bar, playing with a pen or something. Got himself a tropical drink. He's looking a little melancholy. And nervous."

"That right?" the boss said.

Devine, who was from Tennessee, loved the boss's hard-ass southern voice, the power in it. It reminded him of a backwoods Baptist minister, perpetually on the verge of going all fire-and-brimstone on his congregation.

"Well, he's going to be singing the blues all right. You just make sure you don't join him for a few. He slips away again, it's your ass."

Devine winced. He didn't take criticism well. Especially from one of the few people he respected.

"So, plan is still in place?" Devine said. "Hit him when he goes back to his room?"

"Yes, Devine. You remembered from five minutes ago. Bravo," said the boss. "But if a chance comes up right there in the bar, if you can be discreet, you take it. That's why I sent you in instead of Toporski. You know how to improvise."

Devine shook his head as the boss hung up. He'd never heard the man so tense, so—dare he say it—nervous. Pretty Boy had him rattled. Had them all rattled.

That's why they were up in New York now, all of them. There was a team a short block west in front of a gym on 67th and Amsterdam, and another outside the hotel.

They had Pretty Boy boxed in once and for all.

"El Jefe still got his boxers in a wad, eh?" said Therkelson.

"Yep," Devine said as he glanced over at the blond, middle linebacker–sized Therkelson. His big iron Swede thumbs were flying on his Galaxy, playing some game. "You know, Therk, you got a real funny way of conducting surveillance with your face in that phone."

"Ah," Therkelson said, not even glancing up. "You got it covered. I'm the muscle here in our little partnership, Timmy. Be wrong not to let you do anything. I want to make sure a little guy like you feels like you're contributing."

THREE

DEVINE MUNCHED A handful of complimentary jalapeño peanuts as he kept his eyes trained on the target.

He didn't know how they'd tracked Pretty Boy down. A few of the guys were saying the boss man had an old friend in the NSA, which seemed valid. With access to phone and credit card tracking, you could pinpoint any old Tom, Dick, or Harry in the civilized part of the planet in half an hour.

And *what* Pretty Boy was doing, they didn't know that, either. All they knew was that it wasn't part of the playbook. He'd bugged out for a little R&R for the long weekend like the rest of them, but then come Tuesday, he didn't show up. No word.

That was a week ago. Now they'd finally run him down, here in New York in this fancy Pajama Boy gin mill, of all places.

Devine watched as the hot bartender tossed Pretty Boy another interested glance. *Had a woman, even an ugly one, ever looked at him like that?* he thought. No. Not even when he gave them the money first. The bitter inequities of the world.

Yeah, Devine thought, nodding as he looked at Pretty Boy. He was going to enjoy this little piece of work.

It was about three minutes later when Pretty Boy put down his empty glass and stood up. He was heading toward the can. Devine had been monitoring it. There was no one in there.

Welcome to an evening at the improv, Devine thought as he suddenly slapped the phone into Therkelson's lap.

"C'mon," he said, already moving as he watched Pretty Boy push open the restroom door.

He sent Therkelson in by himself while he watched the hall to keep out any civilians. He heard some scuffling behind the door, a muffled grunt. Therkelson knew his orders. Neutralize him, then do a strip search if necessary.

He waited a full minute, checking his stainless steel Rolex, and then another.

What the hell was taking him so long? Devine thought.

He couldn't take it anymore. He pushed open the door.

And came face to face with the shocking and unthinkable.

Therkelson, the incredible Therk himself, was lying unmoving, facedown on the white tile.

As if that weren't enough, as Devine stood there still gaping in wide wonder, one of the stall doors slammed open and cracked him right in the forehead.

An instant later came a searing pain in his neck as Pretty Boy hit him with Therkelson's stun gun for a buzzing moment. Devine threw up jalapeño peanuts all over himself when Pretty

Boy savagely kneed him in the balls. Several times, lightning-quick, like a Thai boxer.

Before he knew it, Devine was down next to Therkelson on his hands and knees like a baby, seeing stars in the tile work. Pretty Boy leapt him like a track hurdle and exited.

Palming himself up from his own vomit a few dazed and throbbing minutes later, Devine shook his head as he fished out his phone.

Here we go again, he thought as he dialed the boss man.

FOUR

THE MAN IN black was a serious runner. He ran seventy miles a week on a strict plan. He did tempo runs and speed training. He didn't just run 5Ks, he usually won them.

But he was gasping like a day-one Biggest Loser and had sweated clean through the back of his suit jacket by the time he came up the sixteen flights of steps and burst from the stairwell door out onto the hotel's roof deck.

He scanned the deck. Dark blue-black sky and cold air. Rattan couches under string lights. A gas fire pit turned off now. No people. No team. They weren't up here. At least not yet.

He thought he could find a way out the back of the hotel, but there was only the stairwell. There was no way he could have gone out the front. If Devine and Therkelson were here, they were all here, strung out in a perimeter.

He was in a slipknot now, which was tightening as he stood there.

Beyond the fire pit, there was an enclosed rooftop bar with a Reserved sign on a stand in front of its French doors. Through the glass, he could see guests and wait staff and tables set with flowers and white linens. A DJ in a tuxedo shirt bent by a turntable, and then there was a sudden blast of swinging trumpets and Sinatra singing "Come Dance with Me."

Clueless civilians. No help in that direction. No time to even ask.

He went to the roof's edge and looked down on Broadway. Sixteen stories down. Two lanes of moving traffic. Lights of Lincoln Center. Some people on the sidewalk. No way to tell the good guys from the bad guys.

He rushed along the roof deck, skirting the building's perimeter to 67th Street, looking for a fire escape. At the northeastern edge of the building down 67th, he was hoping for another building he could escape onto, but there was nothing except a huge empty dirt lot with a bunch of construction equipment.

He'd come along the southeastern back corner of the hotel when he finally saw his out.

Behind the hotel was an old building under renovation. They were doing brickwork and had an outside scaffold set up, a cruciform track running from roof to ground with a movable scaffold forming the horizontal part of the cross. The right-hand end of the scaffold was about fifteen feet away from where he was standing, and about a floor and a half below the level of the hotel roof.

He looked behind him at the path he'd just come down. If he went back to the other edge of the hotel by 67th, ran full-out and got a little height as he leapt off the top of the waist-high wall, he could do it. He could long jump it.

Don't think. Don't look down. Just do it.

He made it to the other end of the roof deck and had turned back for his running start when Therkelson came out of the shadow on his right and grabbed him.

Forgetting his knife, the dark-haired man scrambled with animal panic to break the bigger, stronger man's iron grip. He bashed the big son of a bitch in his mouth with the heel of his right hand, trying to get a thumb in his eye with his left.

But Therkelson didn't let go.

Gripping the struggling dark-haired man by his lapels, Therkelson lifted him up off his feet and, without preamble, easily and silently threw him hard off the side of the building.

In that first terrible instant out in the black space and open cold air, the dark-haired man saw the city around him, like an upside-down I♥NY postcard snapshot. Window lights and water towers and the setbacks on the apartment buildings.

Then he was spinning and falling, the cold air rushing and ripping in his eyes and face.

No, no, no! Can't, can't! Not now! he thought over the blasting of the air and his heart, as he free-fell faster and faster through the cold and black—down, down, down.

FIVE

AT THE BARRIER to the construction site, Devine ripped a piece of plywood free and rushed in.

The place was empty and unlit. He pulled the wood back into place and scurried along the wall of the hotel, searching the concrete-dusted iron pipes, snarls of cable, and mounds of brick rubble and ash-gray dirt.

He glanced up at the buildings around him. Three hundred and sixty degrees of endless windows, in rows and columns. Had somebody seen?

As if. The phone-faced folks of this metropolis didn't so much as look up while walking across the damn street these days. The chance of some Jimmy Stewart type laid up with a broken leg at a window witnessing Pretty Boy's Superman audition was as about as remote as him surviving his assisted sixteen-story swan dive.

Welcome to New York City, Devine thought as he walked around a pallet of cinder blocks. Apathy central. Home of eight and a half million ways to not give a shit whether another human being lives or dies.

He found Pretty Boy on the other side of the battered steel tower of a pile driver, between some orange netting and a bunch of empty spackle buckets. He was on his back, blood covering his face.

Devine looked down and clicked his penlight. Oh my. The worksite wasn't the only thing that needed reconstruction. Pretty Boy wasn't looking too pretty anymore, that was for sure. Devine looked around; he must have hit the steel housing on the pile driver on his way down.

As he knelt beside the body, he realized that, unbelievably, Pretty Boy was still breathing. Devine lifted his wrist and expertly took his pulse. Very, very faint. But still there, for the moment.

"You did this to yourself, you stupid ass. You know I'm right," Devine said as he searched him. "You screwed yourself real good, Pretty Boy. What did you think was gonna happen?"

He found some cash in his right pants pocket, along with a hotel room card and a little flip knife at the back of his belt. The man's phone was in his inside jacket pocket, and he slid it out. It was still on. The phone was in one of those industrial waterproof shock cases and had survived the fall unharmed. How do you like that?

"Who says they don't make good products anymore?" Devine said as he pocketed it.

He patted Pretty Boy down, took off his shoes and socks, and unbuckled his belt. He did a quick professional groin probe with his green rubber-gloved hands. There was nothing else on him. Not even a wallet. It had to be on his phone then, on his contacts or in his notes. It wasn't in his room. They'd already checked there. No luck. Found what looked liked a couple of grand in cash, sure—but left it. Give the cops a chance to chase their tails.

Devine shook his head as he took Pretty Boy's pulse again. Still alive, the stupid ass. Too dumb to die. Was he conscious on some level?

"Where is it?" he said to him. "On your phone, right? Is it on your phone? Tell me, bro, and I'll save you. You still have a chance."

He waited. Nothing. He looked at the state of him. His face and jaw. Pretty Boy couldn't have talked if he'd wanted to.

"Okay, have it your way," Devine said, pinching Pretty Boy's nose and closing a hand over his mouth.

Devine clucked his tongue and shook his head down at Pretty Boy as he made the smallest groan of protest.

"No, Pretty Boy, it's time for me to talk," Devine told him quietly as he squatted there, killing him.

"See, everybody always said how top-notch you were. Mr. True Team Member, grace under pressure and all that jazz, but I never bought it. I never liked you. I always knew you looked down on me, that it was just an act.

"You had it all, bro. But you had to go and screw yourself up and ruin everything. We're all really disappointed in you, man.

Me and Therk and the boss. You had such potential, dude, such amazing potential, but you blew it like the loser that you deep down are and always were. Okay? I just wanted you to know that. Get it off my chest and set the record straight. I feel better now. Thanks a bunch, bro. Good night now."

CHASE

CHAPTER 1

"GOOD MORNING, DETECTIVE BENNETT."

A little after 8:30 on a Tuesday morning late in October, I smiled at the double row of kids sitting cross-legged on the linoleum at the front of the classroom. They were seven-year-olds, about thirty of them, very cute and trying to stay still so as not to muss their Catholic school uniforms.

I was doing a little free PR work for the NYPD. It was Holy Name's career day, and I was there in front of my youngest daughter, Chrissy's, second grade class.

It wasn't the first time I had spoken at the school. In fact, I had spoken at the second grade career day for pretty much all of my ten adopted kids.

But because of my not-so-stellar track record as a speaker, I'd already been told by my older daughters to keep my talk brief and to the point. There was to be no going off script, and there would be absolutely no displays of the patented Bennett sense of humor.

I had absolutely no idea what they were talking about. My kids were far too sensitive.

I took a breath and Chrissy's teacher, Sr. Claire, smiled at me encouragingly.

"Try to keep the f-bombs to a minimum, Serpico, would you, please?" whispered my grandfather, Father Seamus, who was at my side to observe the proceedings. "Try not to scar the minds of these fine young Christians any more than necessary."

"I'll do my best, Monsignor. Thanks for the pep talk. It means a lot coming from a man of the cloth."

Seamus was my actual grandfather and, yes, a priest. He'd gone into the seminary after Nana passed. Though well into his eighties, he was still as sharp and sarcastic as ever.

"Hello, boys and girls. I'm Chrissy's dad, and I'm a police officer. Who knows what police officers do?" I started.

A cute, nerdy little kid with glasses, Henry, raised his hand from the back.

"Yes, Henry?"

"Have you ever handled a sniper rifle?" he said as the other kids started laughing.

"Well, yes, actually. I have. Now who knows what a policeman does?"

Just as I said this, my phone started ringing. I had forgotten to put it on airplane mode, and the loud tones started playing, to the amusement of all the kids.

Naturally, one of my kids at home had set it onto the stupidest ring available in the settings, a doofy electronic ditty called "By the Seaside." As I unsuccessfully tried to hit the right button to shut it off, Henry leapt up with an impromptu belly dance for his buddies. Thanks, Henry.

As the chaos erupted, I looked down at my phone screen and saw that the call was from Chief Fabretti, my boss. Which was actually a little concerning. He didn't call me unless there was something happening.

"Hey, Sr. Claire," I said, waving my phone. "I'm sorry. I actually have to take this."

"Please, Detective. Take it, by all means," she said, settling Henry back into his place on the floor.

Leaving, I glanced back and saw Chrissy covering her face in abject embarrassment. Great.

"Another fine speaking engagement, Tony Robbins," Father Seamus said, giving me a mock thumbs-up as I left. "But don't worry, I'll cover for you."

I shook my head as my stage Irishman of a grandfather rushed to the front of the class and cleared his throat elaborately.

"Boys and girls and girls and boys. Please allow me to introduce myself. My name is Father Seamus," he said, taking a bow as the door closed behind me.

CHAPTER 2

TWENTY MINUTES LATER, I was on 67th Street between Broadway and Columbus, standing in front of a beeping Caterpillar front loader as it was about to drop a bunch of rubble into a curbside dump truck. Inside the hollowed-out dirt worksite behind it, I could see yellow crime-scene tape cordoning off a section to the right.

"Hey! Hold it right there! Back it up!" I yelled to the hard hat in the cab, showing him my shield.

"What the hell is this?" said a big guy, who looked like the contractor in charge. He rushed over and got in my face. "What's the problem? We're working on the other side, away from the body. The first officer said it was okay."

"The first officer was wrong," I said, stepping up till we were practically forehead to forehead. "I'm the responding detective. This entire site is a crime scene. Nothing gets moved out of it. In fact, you and everybody else get out on the sidewalk until I say different."

"Are you mad?" the contractor said, in his thick Brooklyn accent. "We're on a schedule. Cement is on its way. We're pouring in less than an hour."

"Not anymore," I told him as I walked toward the crime-scene tape.

"Hey, Detective. Sorry about that," said a young black sergeant, stepping up beside me as I arrived at the crime scene. "I thought it would be all right since they wanted to work on the other side of the site. Besides, the guy looks like he fell or jumped."

"Looks can be deceiving, Sergeant," I said. "Please go out on the sidewalk and keep those people off my back."

"Hey, Mike. Long time, no see," said a sharp crime-scene tech I knew, Judy Yelas, who was photographing the body. "What brings the legendary Major Case to the lowly West Side? I thought the Twentieth Precinct was handling."

"Me, too, until my boss called," I said with a shrug.

"Ah, I see. Orders from on high. Poli-tricks as usual," Judy said, rolling her eyes.

Poli-tricks was actually kind of right.

As it turned out, Index House, the hotel beside the crime scene, kept appearing in the headlines for all the wrong reasons. Open for only six months, it had received negative publicity for a couple of viral videos. One was of people having sex on a balcony. Another was of a famous NFL player drunkenly knocking out a woman in an elevator.

It also turned out that the owner of the hotel was a

wealthy political contributor and close family friend of the new governor. Now, the powers that be wanted to "figure out" this latest Big Apple hospitality fiasco as quickly and discreetly as possible.

I don't know about any of that wishful sort of political thinking. Nor, frankly, do I care. A person was dead, and I was available, so here I was.

I came around the pile driver and squatted down on my heels to look at the body. The deceased was a tall, lean, dark-haired man in his early thirties, maybe. He wore a nice dark suit and was positioned lying on his back in a pool of blood, his face smashed up horribly.

I took a few steps back, looked up at the hotel and unintentionally let out a whistle. He must have come down face-first and hit the metal pile driver on the right, which flipped him like a rag doll. I felt terrible for the guy. Like pretty much every other jumper I had ever dealt with, he seemed to have suffered a gruesome death.

"Wallet? Phone?" I said to Judy.

"None that I can see. I didn't pat him down, though. Thought you'd want to."

I knelt beside him, pulled on a pair of rubber gloves, and went through the pockets of his pants and jacket. There was nothing. No wallet, no phone. Not even when Judy helped me turn him and look underneath the body.

Didn't make a lot of sense. Drunk? I thought. Suicide? But I let my conclusions slide for the time being, and snapped a few pictures with my phone of this poor citizen's ruined face.

"I'm done here, Judy," I said, giving her my card. "When the medical examiner gets here, tell him this gentleman is good to go."

"That's it, huh?" Judy said, smiling. "Love 'em and leave 'em? Mike Bennett, NYPD's version of the Lone Ranger. Who was that masked man?"

"Hey, feel free to take notes on what an efficient textbook investigation looks like," I said with a wink. "Like you said, you're dealing with the legendary Major Case."

CHAPTER 3

THE FIRST THING I noticed as I entered the stylish modern hotel off the 67th Street sidewalk were the two people talking by the front desk.

One was a twenty-something white guy wearing an Arab keffiyeh scarf with his blue blazer. The other was an elegant middle-aged black woman in a plum-colored dress and pearls. They seemed to be arguing quietly, and the guy in the scarf was holding up his phone between them, right in the lady's face.

"Hi. I'm Detective Bennett. Are you the hotel manager?" I said to the woman.

"Yes. I'm Amanda Milton," she said pleasantly. I stepped between them, almost knocking the phone out of the guy's hand.

"And who are you?" I said to the guy curtly. As if I didn't know.

"Luke Messerly. From the *New York Times,*" he said.

"Could I talk to you for a sec, Luke?" I said. I steered him toward the front revolving door. "I just got here, buddy," I said in a low tone. "I need to get a handle on this investigation. Give me your card, and as soon as I have something, I'll get back to you. I promise."

"Yeah, right. Don't give me the runaround, Detective. I know who you are. You're Mike Bennett, the NYPD's go-to Major Case problem solver. Or is it fixer? I also know that the owner of this hotel is very good friends with the governor. Coincidence? I think not."

I smiled as I put an arm over Luke's shoulder.

"Luke, you're quick. I like that. But listen. Your boss told you to drop everything and rush the hell down here, am I right?" I asked.

"Of course. What does that have to do with anything?"

"Luke, we're in the same boat, buddy. My boss did the same exact thing to me."

"Which means?"

"Which means we're in this together. But if you start stepping on my toes, then how can I be nice to you and help you keep your new job? See, I know you're young and impatient, Luke. I was the same way myself once upon a time. But if you continue to push, I will 'no comment' you straight back to the real estate or Queens section you just came from. You don't want that, do you? Of course not. You're in the bigs now, Luke. The last thing you want is to get sent back down, right?"

"I guess," he said. I slapped my card into his hand and nudged him into the exit.

"Let's cooperate, buddy, and truly, we'll all get through this just fine," I said with a smile, as I helped the doorman push the reporter out the door.

CHAPTER 4

"FROM WHAT TIME do you need the footage?" said the hotel's stocky Asian security head, Albert Yoon, a couple of minutes later as I stood in his tiny basement office.

"We'll start at around four o'clock last evening," I said, as I stood watching his computer screen. "You have two bars, right? Any trouble last night?"

"Not really," Yoon said in a Long Island accent. He had been a Suffolk County cop. "Someone upchucked in the men's restroom in the lobby. No precedent set there."

"Wait. Stop it there," I said. I saw a tall black-haired guy in a dark suit on the screen checking in. "That might be him. Can you match the check-in time to the name?"

"We sure can," Yoon said, clicking open a new screen. "Let's see. Your guy is one Pete Mitchell. He's still checked in. He's in 717."

"Any charges on his credit card?" I said as I wrote it down.

"No. It says there's no credit card. He pre-paid for the room in cash."

"Did he show ID?"

"Yeah. The desk clerk should have a photocopy of it upstairs. Anyone who pays in cash has to show valid ID in case a room gets trashed or what have you."

Yoon was standing but suddenly sat back down.

"Wait a second," he said. He clicked the security video again and hit Fast-forward. "I think this guy, Mitchell, might be the guy who yakked in the men's room. Look at this."

Yoon brought up the shot of the lobby hall, and I watched as Mitchell headed into what I assumed to be the men's room. A moment later, two other men appeared in the hall, one of them entering while the other waited. Some time passed, and the other guy in the hall went into the restroom and then Mitchell reappeared.

"See the kind of nervous look on his face and how he hurries away?"

I nodded. "Where does he go? Can you see?" I asked.

Yoon clicked on another screen, and we watched as Mitchell pulled open another door at the end of the hall.

"That leads to the B stairwell. There are no cameras in there. Maybe he went back to his room? I'll look at the camera on seven."

Yoon changed screens and clicked the mouse several times.

"That's funny," he said. "The camera on seven is broken or something. It's not showing anything."

I looked at Yoon.

"Does the stairwell go all the way up to the roof?" I said.

Yoon looked back at me.

"It does go all the way," he said.

"That's when he did it," I said. "He went all the way up the stairs and jumped off."

CHAPTER 5

I FINALLY ARRIVED back at my apartment that night around five.

A message on the fridge said Mary Catherine was out to get the twins from cheerleading practice and Ricky from soccer, and instructed me to put the lasagnas in the fridge into the oven at 5:30. Bennett situation normal, I thought as I cracked open a can of Corona Light and took a gulp. Busier than the control tower at LaGuardia.

Mary Catherine is my kids' nanny, and also my girlfriend. I'm a widower, so it isn't as sleazy as it sounds. Or maybe it is; I'm not an expert on these things. At least that's what I tell myself whenever my Catholic guilt taps me on the shoulder.

"Dad! Look, look! It came! It came!" My daughter Shawna rushed at me with a large tan envelope as I walked into the living room. It was from the Schenectady Chamber of Commerce. There were half a dozen pamphlets inside, as well as the *Daily Gazette* newspaper.

"Mary Catherine said after dinner I can cut out some of the pictures for the poster board."

"Hey, that's awesome, Shawna."

"No, it's not, Dad," said Trent, coming in behind her with his arms crossed. "It's not fair that Miss Goody Two-shoes got all this great stuff for the project and I didn't get anything. Mine's filled with just stupid printouts off the internet."

Oh, no. Here we go again, I thought, sharing a smile with Eddie, who was on the couch simultaneously reading a paperback and watching ESPN with the sound off.

With ten adopted kids, drama on the home front is to be expected. The latest brouhaha concerned two of my youngest, Shawna and Trent, who were in the same fourth grade class and were both doing projects about New York State.

Competitively, of course. Shawna was assigned the city of Schenectady, a metropolis whose factoids we had been regaled with for the last two weeks.

Trent had nearby Rome, New York, which—in addition to being the place where the country's first cheese factory was founded—was the nation's current 140th largest city.

Who knew? We did. That was who. Whether we wanted to or not. No one was in a more rabid New York state of mind than the Bennetts.

"Hey, look, guys. Quick. On TV. Look there," Eddie said, pointing quickly at some news footage of a car on fire. "This is just in. Schenectady and Rome, New York, just both suddenly exploded. They're both gone, and now your projects are gonna really totally stink. Darn. I'm so sorry."

"D-A-A-D!!!" Shawna and Trent yelled in unison.

CHAPTER 6

AFTER PUTTING ALL fighters back into their respective corners, D-A-A-D had to make a call from his bedroom.

"Hey, Chief. It's Mike," I said to Fabretti.

"Mike, please tell me some good news on this jumper," he said. "My boss keeps calling me every five minutes."

"Okay, here we go," I said, putting my beer on my nightstand as I fished out my notepad. "Seven o'clock yesterday, a thirty-something male in a dark silk suit checks into the Index House Hotel under the name of Pete Mitchell, pays in cash, and shows them ID."

"What do you mean, under the name of?"

"Turns out, this ID, a Delaware driver's license, is a fake. There actually are a number of Pete Mitchells who live in Delaware, but based on age alone, it's pretty clear that none of them are our dead guy. His license is a good fake, though."

"Oh, here we go. No ID. An actual suicide whodunit?" Fabretti said.

"That's not all. This guy gets a room, drops off his stuff, comes back down and has a drink at the bar. About ten minutes after that, he goes to the restroom and blows chunks. Then he goes up to the roof through the stairwell, and they find him the next morning in the worksite beside the hotel."

"What?"

"Exactly. Weird, but it gets weirder. In a drawer in his room, there's one of those fanny packs. The fake ID is in the pack along with a ton of cash in twenties and fifties, almost ten grand altogether. Beside the pack is a box of condoms in a CVS bag and that's it. No luggage, no deodorant, no tighty-whities. Nothing."

"So you're saying our guy is some kind of John Doe?"

"Yep. Even the Pete Mitchell name seems like a fake. I looked it up online. It's the name of Tom Cruise's character in *Top Gun*."

"How does this make sense? He's a drug dealer or something? Grabs some prophylactics and hits the Big Apple for a night in funky town but instead jumps off the roof? Is that the way you're leaning? He jumped, right?"

"I'm about seventy-five percent there. But with this guy's fishy ID and the dough in his room and the fact there's no video on the roof, we can't be positive yet."

"Medical examiner run his prints?"

"In process. Still waiting to hear. You know latent prints at the ME's office. It's a bottleneck unless they get some heat. Especially if it looks like a suicide."

"All right, I'll make some calls there. Hit me the second you hear about the prints. By the way, how does the press look on this one? Any more rabid than usual?"

I frowned as I held my phone. This is the kind of stuff I'm always leery of in Major Case. I am a cop, I felt like reminding him. My job is to solve homicides, not to do PR errand-boy work for politicians and the rich, connected people who financed their campaigns.

"Not that I really noticed, Chief," I fibbed, and hung up.

CHAPTER 7

AT TEN FIFTEEN the next morning, I walked through the front doors of the office of the Chief Medical Examiner on East 26th and First Avenue.

With its low ceiling and rows of stark blue metal tables, the autopsy room at the back of the first floor always reminded me of a pool hall—the least-fun game hall of all time.

The tables were thankfully empty this morning. Doing my best not to peek into the lab's scales and buckets and glass-doored fridges, I crossed the white-tiled room to the office of Assistant Medical Examiner Dr. Clarissa Linder.

Dr. Linder was a genial, nice-looking woman with short dark-blond hair. I'd worked cases with her before. Before becoming an ME, she had a lucrative pediatrician practice on the Upper East Side. But when she'd turned forty, inspired to do something more challenging, she had traded in Band-Aids and lollipops for psycho killers and floaters.

Her door was open and she was standing behind her desk, thumbing at the Fitbit on her wrist.

"You have one of these stupid fitness things, Mike?" she said. "They're addictive. If you have nine hundred steps, you find yourself walking in circles around the room just to get to a thousand."

"No, I don't," I said, and sat in the chair in front of her desk. "But I'm certainly no stranger to walking around in circles. Speaking of which, what's going on with Mr. Mitchell? Or I suppose Mr. Doe is probably more appropriate. Unless we've heard from latent prints?"

She raised an eyebrow as she handed me her file.

"No such luck on the prints, Mike. As usual, the wheels of death processing grind slowly."

"So what's your take on Mr. Doe?"

"Where do I begin?" she said. "Did you see the amazing shape of this guy?"

"He did seem pretty trim. Worked out some, did he?"

"He looks like an Olympian. Jacked, as the kids say, with a body fat percentage in the single digits."

I shook my head. This case just kept getting weirder.

"Anything else? Cause of death was the fall, right?"

"Yep. Massive bruising and impact contusions on the skin and muscle, especially to the head and upper chest. The bones in his face were completely pulverized."

"Anything in his bloodstream that would have made a healthy person like him suddenly want to throw himself off a roof? Like flakka or something? Crystal meth? We have some indication that he might have thrown up prior to the fall."

"No, nothing," she said, surprised. "A little alcohol in his blood was all. You think he threw up? I don't know about that. He had food in his stomach."

"Is that so?"

"Yep," Dr. Linder said. "Food and this."

She lifted a plastic evidence bag on her desk beside the autopsy report. There were two items inside of it. One of them was yellowish and thin and looked like a deflated balloon. The other item looked like a thin slip of paper.

"What the hell is this?" I said. "How was this in the guy's stomach? A piece of paper in a condom?"

"With numbers written on it," the doctor said. "They seem random. I counted them twice. There are twenty-four of them altogether."

"That's just—"

"Yep," Dr. Linder said.

"Like the way people sometimes smuggle drugs," I mumbled, turning the bag over in my hand.

"The same exact way," Dr. Linder said. "Have you ever seen something like this, Mike? Because this is a first for me."

CHAPTER 8

"SO TELL ME, Una. Mary Catherine was a nut when you guys were teens back in Tipperary, wasn't she? Remember, I'm a cop, so don't try to lie. I'm highly trained in the art of truth detection."

"How did you know, Mike?" said Una, a very funny, heavyset forty-something with long black hair. "Oh, Mike, she was just mad, so she was. Closing down discos, out-drinking full rugby teams, all the lads chasing her. She was a sheer panic of a woman, a true holy terror in high heels."

"I knew it," I said and smiled at Mary, blue-eyed and blushing beside me in the van.

I was driving down Broadway in Midtown, on chauffeur duty for Mary and Una, her cousin visiting from Ireland. They were going to see the new musical *School of Rock* at the Winter Garden Theatre, then to drinks and a late dinner at my good buddy Emmett O'Lunney's joint across the street. I'd already called ahead and told Emmett to pull out all the stops, the full red carpet treatment. Not so much for Una, but for Mary, our house martyr. The kids had insisted that she enjoy herself without us in her hair for once, on a much-deserved girls' night out.

I stole a glance at Mary again. So heart-swellingly pretty, done up in makeup and a little black dress. I remembered a line from an old drunk cop at a retirement party I'd taken her to over the holidays.

"Your wife, Mike," the former emergency services cop said, with a drunkenly wistful and old-fashioned earnestness, "your wife is an Irish beauty."

I'll say, I thought, as I watched Mary blush even more under my gaze. Though, technically, she wasn't my wife.

And why not, Bennett? You complete idiot! came my interior Catholic. Funny how he always sounded sort of like Grandfather Seamus.

"Penny for your thoughts," Mary whispered, squeezing my hand as Una took a call on her cell behind us. "As if I don't know."

"You want to know what I'm thinking about right now? You really want to know?" I whispered back.

"Yes," she said.

"I'm thinking about dropping Una off at the next corner," I said.

"And then?" she said, stifling a giggle.

"What are you two whispering about up there?" Una called out. "I'm not interrupting anything, I hope."

"Una, we were merely conferring about how best to honor

your visit here, upon the shores of this fabulous free and just land," I said, gesturing at the insane snarl of traffic. "Mary thought the Empire State Building might be nice, but I said no. We first must book you some ice time at the Rockefeller Center rink."

"Oh, was that it?" Una said. Mary gave me a wink.

"I may not be as highly trained in the art of truth detection as you, Mike," Una said after a beat. "But we from the Emerald Isle do know a little something about ripe blarney."

CHAPTER 9

THE NEXT DAY I was back at Holy Name, doing my best to dodge basketballs and screaming grammar school tweens during lunch yard duty when I got a call on my cell phone from an unknown number.

"Hello, Detective. My name is Len Brimer. I write for the *Daily News*. I was given your number by a woman from your squad."

"Yeah, sorry, Len," I said, as I pulled my old friend hyperactive Henry down from where he was trying to climb the yard's chain-link fence. "No comment for now. I'm still trying to run down some leads."

"No, you don't understand. I'm not calling as a reporter. I'm actually involved in the case. At least, maybe. That jumper from the hotel? I think I was on my way to meet him before he died."

"What do you mean, you think?"

"It's a kind of a long story. We should meet."

Twenty minutes later, I got out of my unmarked Chevy on 30th near Eighth, where several huge flocks of pigeons were dive-bombing between the old concrete office buildings of south Midtown.

Before Alfred Hitchcock could show up, I crossed the sidewalk to a Garment District pub called The Liffey. Brimer showed up a little later. He was a tall dude, six four, six five; in his thirties; balding but athletic-looking. Wearing black wind pants and a gray Hofstra hoodie, he looked like a basketball coach.

"Okay, Detective, here's what happened," Len Brimer began after we were seated in a booth. "So I'm out at Citi Field trying to get in to see the general manager about the Campbell trade, and I get a call. The guy calls himself Charlie, and he tells me he's an old friend of my younger brother, Adam. He tells me he was in Adam's frat at Syracuse ten years ago, and that Adam had told him about me. That I was a reporter or whatever."

"That sounds weird enough," I said as the waitress brought me a Bud Light pint.

"It gets weirder," Brimer said. "So this guy, Charlie, said he had a huge story about the government that he wanted to tell the press, but that he didn't know anyone in New York or trust any reporters. He said he knew Adam was a great guy and that he had spoken highly of me so he was wondering if I could help him."

"A huge story about the government? Like a whistle-blower sort of thing?" I said.

"He was vague, but that was the kind of gist I got," Brimer said, nodding. "I told him that really wasn't my bag, and I could refer him to some good guys I knew, but he said no. That it had to be me. And also not to tell a soul. He was adamant about that. He sounded pretty paranoid."

"Did he have any sort of accent? From New York, you think?"

"Maybe not New York, but he sounded normal. Like anybody. Definitely American. He sounded sane but worked up, so I finally said okay, and we set up a meeting at Index House on the West Side."

"Then what happened?"

"So I go there and nothing. He told me he was a tall guy with black hair, but as I head into the bar where he said to meet, I don't see him. I talked to the bartender. She said she remembered him, but he left. I even spoke to the desk clerk to see if he'd left a message. But there was nothing."

"What time did you get there?"

"9:40. 9:50."

"Yeah, we think he was already dead by then."

"I knew it," Brimer said, scrunching his face as he stared down at the table. "I tell ya, I feel like crap. Instead of heading straight there, I waited for the Mets' GM and then the cab in from Flushing got stuck in traffic. Then when I heard about the jumper, I thought, wait a second, was it this guy who called me?"

"Did you speak to your brother about any Charlie in his frat?"

"I did. Adam knew lots of people in his frat, he's still in contact with a bunch of them on Facebook and LinkedIn, but he can't think of anyone named Charlie."

So now our mystery man was some kind of whistle-blower?

I looked out the window, watching the birds looping above Eighth, my mind turning over the false names and the twenty-four numbers in the man's stomach.

CHAPTER 10

DEVINE SAT IN the backseat of the rental Nissan truck on Eighth, staring out the tinted back window at the bar that the cop had gone into. He might have seen him at the window, but it was pretty foggy.

It didn't matter. Therkelson was on it. He had gone in five minutes after him and recorded the cop and reporter's whole convo with the shotgun mike in his duffel bag. Devine had listened in, and he was pretty pumped. Because overall, it seemed like they were good. That Pretty Boy had contacted a reporter could have been very bad, but they had taken him out in time. The reporter didn't know anything, and neither, apparently, did the clueless cop.

They had even found what they were looking for on the notes on Pretty Boy's phone. The green light was staying green. The Pretty Boy problem had been solved. The boss man was going to like this little turn of events.

Devine smiled as he took another dainty, savoring spoonful of the fig-and-goat-milk ice cream they'd gotten from a trendy place on East Broadway, Ice & Vice.

He'd bought the latest Zagat's foodie guide when they got into town. When they weren't working, he and Therkelson had been hitting all the newest and coolest eateries. Dinner was going to be parrilladas mixtas from some happening Tex-Mex joint called Javelina in Union Square. He couldn't wait.

He knew a little about food. How to actually prepare and cook it instead of just ramming it into your piehole like mail into a mailbox, the way Therkelson did. Growing up, his grandfather owned the second-best diner in Dyersburg, Tennessee. By thirteen, he was working behind the flat top, cracking eggs two at a time for the truck drivers and line workers from the stove factory just across the interstate.

Might have been a cook. Maybe even a frou-frou New York jackhole celebrity one. Except Pop-Pop died and his grandma sold The Spoon—officially called the Wood N Spoon Diner, but everybody just called it The Spoon.

Therkelson opened the door and got into the driver's seat in a hurry. "Hey, snap out of it, Devine," he said, starting the truck.

"We got movement. They're coming out. Should we follow the reporter or the cop?"

"The cop, of course," Devine said, scraping ice cream off the wax cup. "Stay on the cop. The reporter doesn't know his ass from his elbow."

CHAPTER 11

FOLLOWING MY AFTERNOON meeting with Len Brimer, I went back to the Major Case squad room. Parked in my cubicle, I was drinking a Diet Mountain Dew and polishing off the last crumbs of a Cronut when I received an email from the hotel with the additional footage I had requested.

With the new whistle-blower angle Brimer had told me about still fresh in my mind, I wanted to take a closer look at the other two guys who'd been in the bathroom with our mysterious John Doe.

I watched the video over and over again. John Doe goes in, followed by a big blond dude and a shorter guy with dark hair. The short guy waits in the hall. As I looked more carefully, I noticed the short guy in the hall checked his watch twice before going in. I also noticed the way he was standing in the hall, head slowly swiveling back and forth like a guard or a sentry. As if maybe he knew that his big buddy was dealing with John Doe and was making sure no one intervened.

After John Doe came out, the expression on his face might

not have been embarrassment at throwing up, but panic after barely fighting off two attackers. The two guys who came out about a minute after him didn't look too beat-up, I saw, as I let the tape run on. But the quick, determined way they split, the short one going to the front desk and elevator bank as the other bigger guy headed up the back stairwell following John Doe, was definitely of note.

About seven minutes later, the big blond guy came back out of the rear stairwell, met up with the short guy, and then they left.

I thought about that. Two men go into the back stairwell that leads to the roof and only one leaves seven minutes later? I couldn't say for sure if the blond guy had thrown our John Doe off the roof, but I couldn't rule it out.

I was still sitting there letting these new concerns sink in when my desk phone rang with a muffled chirp.

"Mike, I don't know how you jumped the line," Medical Examiner Dr. Linder said in my ear. "But in my hand, I hold the hot-off-the-press report from our latent lab. Today's your lucky day, Mike. You have a hit on your mystery man jumper."

"Tell me this isn't a practical joke. What's his name?"

"One Stephen Eardley," she said. "It says here, he's in the Air Force. His prints actually came from the FBI database off his 2001 Armed Forces application. I'll email the whole report to you just as soon as I'm done scanning it."

"You're the best. I owe you, Clarissa. Talk to you later," I said, already bringing up a search engine to find Stephen Eardley.

As soon as I hit Enter, my jaw fell open. I collapsed back into my office chair in wide-eyed wonder as the search results continued.

I didn't think this case could get any stranger, but it had.

I clicked the first link and read a news article from the Ogden, Utah, *Standard-Examiner* dated May 20, 2007.

LOCAL HERO DIES IN IRAQ

The small town of Liberty in northwestern Ogden Valley is in mourning today as a native son, Air Force pilot Stephen Eardley, was put to rest at the Liberty Cemetery. Eardley, who played football and baseball at Weber High in Pleasant View, was killed in action on Friday, May 3, 2007, when his C-130 aircraft crashed thirty-six minutes after takeoff from Balad Air Base in northern Iraq.

An on-board flight fire that was speculated to have been caused by an electrical short circuit forced Eardley to attempt a crash landing. The pilot was trying to lose altitude quickly in a maneuver known as a side slip when the plane went out of control, inverted, and crashed in the desert. Eardley, a five-year veteran pilot attached to the elite Air Force Special Operations Command, was thirty-two years old.

Killed in action! I thought, as I sat there grabbing the sides of my head. How? How the heck could that be?

How could Eardley be killed in action in a plane crash in the Iraq desert in 2007, and then end up dead again in Midtown Manhattan?

CHAPTER 12

EARLY THE NEXT morning, I was sitting in the crowded business section of a southbound Acela Amtrak train, checking my email between sips of an iced Americano as southern New Jersey streaked past the window beside me.

The high-test coffee was entirely necessary. I'd been up half the night fielding calls as the lid officially blew sheer off the top of my case.

After several phone calls to three different FBI officials of increasing rank, I'd learned that the newspaper article on Eardley was correct. According to Air Force records, Stephen Eardley was KIA in a military plane crash in Iraq in 2007.

Which one would think was nuts enough. But it got more complicated.

Because Eardley had been supposedly killed in a military plane crash in Iraq in '07 during a *classified* mission.

That was why I was heading down to Washington, DC, this rainy gray morning. Since I didn't have intelligence clearance, I was told the best way to make headway into Eardley's death was to contact military intelligence personnel in DC—off the record.

Though a so-called legal Chinese wall separates the intel community from domestic law enforcement, I'd learned that unofficial exceptions are sometimes made for compelling reasons. Especially if there is anonymity and all parties are sufficiently discreet.

Classified intel and Chinese walls, I thought, putting away my phone to look out the train window at the wet trees and old brick factories blurring past. *Deeper and deeper down the rabbit hole, I go.*

Just after ten thirty I got off the train. I found myself smiling despite the rain when I saw the liaison the Bureau had sent to guide me around the Beltway. Waiting in a blue fed car for me, outside the magnificent dripping arches of Union Station, was none other than my good buddy FBI Special Agent Emily Parker.

Parker and I had been on several high-profile cases together, including a series of kidnappings of rich kids up in New York. We'd come close a few times to romantic involvement. It never worked out, yet amazingly, we still liked and talked to each other.

"No bag, I see. Just a briefcase. You pack light," Emily said, after she gave me a hug of greeting.

"Yeah, well, with all the warnings about the stonewalling I'm about to receive from Washington officials, I figured this might be a brief trip."

"Well, we'll see about that, Mike. I've been asking around all morning. I actually have a few leads we can try."

"Has there ever been something like this before, to your knowledge?" I asked as Parker pulled out and cruised us down a busy avenue past the nearby Capitol.

"Something like what?"

"Somebody faking being killed in action, ending up actually alive?"

"Not that I've ever heard of," Emily said. "Desertions, sure, but walking away from a maybe deliberately downed fifty-million-dollar military aircraft? That's a whole different ball of wax."

CHAPTER 13

I THOUGHT WE were going to the Pentagon, across the Potomac, but instead we crossed east over the Anacostia River and headed toward Joint Base Anacostia-Bolling.

Emily explained that our first visit would be with a senior officer in the Defense Intelligence Agency, Chris Milne, a former Marine. The DIA is the military's version of the CIA. If anyone could help us figure out what the hell had happened on a classified Air Force mission, Emily said that Milne, who had done several tours in Iraq with Special Forces, was a pretty good place to start.

Off the highway, we drove along a street lined with beautiful red brick colonial buildings to the checkpoint at the Air Force base visitor's gate.

"NYPD?" a young redheaded Air Force MP said when I flashed my shield. He was carrying an M4. "Let me guess. One of the generals racked himself up a whole lot of parking tickets again?"

"Sorry, soldier. That's classified," I said, cracking a smile.

"I'll bet," he said, letting us through.

We navigated the base's huge campus to reach a low glass corporate-looking building, off by itself near the water.

After another, even more heavy-duty security checkpoint in its lobby, we found ourselves on the fourth floor, sitting in an austere, featureless office with a view. If you craned your neck to the right, you could just see the side of the Washington Monument's towering obelisk across the river.

I was doing just that when Milne walked in, carrying a big white coffee mug with a trailing tea bag tag.

"Emily! Long time, no see," said the tall, balding, Nordic-looking Milne. "How's your daughter? Olivia, right?"

"Olivia, yes. You remembered," Emily said, smiling. "She's fine. Eleven going on twenty. You know the drill. You have four girls, right?"

"Actually, five now."

"Congratulations, Chris. That's awesome. I'd like you to meet Mike Bennett, the detective I was telling you about."

"I have six girls," I said, as we shook hands.

Milne raised an eyebrow.

"And four boys, too," Emily said.

"My goodness. Ten? Busy man. You win, Detective," he said, smiling, as he finally put down his tea and sat. "So what can I do for you folks today?"

It took me a few minutes to explain my crazy case to him. After I was done, he looked at me and then at Emily, and took a long, deliberate sip of his tea.

"So there's no way these prints are somebody else's? No possible way?" he said after a beat.

I shook my head.

"We had three people look at them, including the FBI. It's Eardley."

"Or his clone," Emily said.

"That's simply incredible," Milne said. "He dumps the plane on purpose and then just walks out of Iraq? Why? And nobody picks up on this? What the hell went wrong?"

"That's what we're trying to find out, Chris," Emily said. "See, Eardley's mission was classified. Even the FBI can't access the info. Could you maybe inquire about it for us discreetly?"

"Gee, Emily. I don't know. In '07, a lot of crazy stuff was happening, all directed very sloppily, in my opinion, by the folks at Langley. Something this cuckoo has Foggy Bottom written all over it. I do mostly recruiting now, to be perfectly honest. All this is definitely above my pay grade."

"Foggy Bottom?" I said.

"The State Department, the CIA," Emily said.

"Ah," I said.

"'Ah' is right," Milne said, lifting his mug again. "The CIA means politics."

Poli-tricks, I thought, as the crime scene tech said when I first found Eardley's body.

"We're not looking to jeopardize anybody, of course. We just need a lead here, Chris," Emily said.

"Because actually, Chris, it gets worse," I said, as I took out the video stills of the two guys who were in the bathroom at the hotel. "I don't think Eardley's death was a suicide. I think he was thrown off that hotel. Right before he was about to meet up with a reporter about a government cover-up."

Milne shook his head as he looked at the photos. Then he put down his tea and took a deep breath. After another beat, he let out a low whistle.

"Alrightee, then," he said dismally. "I'll make some phone calls. I'll see what I can do."

CHAPTER 14

CHRIS CAME THROUGH as we were getting into the car. He had been able to arrange a meeting for us at another office, on the other side of the Potomac.

A little after eleven thirty, Emily and I walked through the south parking lot entrance of the Pentagon. Two checkpoints, three massive endless corridors, and an elevator ride later, Air Force Colonel Kristin Payton greeted us by her secretary's desk.

Payton was an outdoorsy-looking woman of about forty-five, pale and raw-boned, with short blond hair. Unlike Chris Milne's office, hers was anything but austere. It had a thick Air Force-blue carpet, a beast of a cherrywood desk, and a comfortable-looking worn leather couch beneath a big double window. A framed article on one of her office's wood-paneled walls revealed that she was one of the first female pilots to fly an A-10 Warthog in combat.

"Mr. Milne has briefed me on what you found up in New York, Detective," Colonel Payton said as she sat us down before her desk. "He also referenced the sensitivity due to the intelligence concerns. Just for the sake of argument, what would you be looking for?"

"Well, I guess finding out how Eardley was designated KIA would be a start. Were there any remains found in the crash?"

"Just off the top of my head, I would say no," Colonel Payton said, folding her hands on her desktop. "Usually the crash of an aircraft as huge as a C-130 will completely obliterate any human remains. If there was an additional fuel fire, which I would assume there was, it would have been even more impossible to recover anything at all. But in all honesty, I don't know. We can't know until we receive and read the AFSC report."

"AFSC?"

"That's Air Force Safety Center, at Kirtland in New Mexico," the colonel said. "It's like the military version of National Transportation Safety. They have to do a report on any and all military aviation incidents."

There was a buzzing sound.

Payton drew a phone from one of her uniform pockets and stood. "Excuse me, please, would you?" she said, and left the room. Emily and I shared a look.

Payton was gone for about three minutes before she hurried back in with a strange, worried look on her taut face. She wiped it off with a deep breath.

"I'm sorry to have to tell you this, but I'm going to have to cancel this meeting. I do not have the authorization to discuss this classified matter with you any further."

"Wait, just like that? Are you kidding, Colonel?" I said.

"No, Detective," she said, giving me a blank, obtuse look. "Do I come across as kidding?"

I took Luke Messerly's card out of my pocket and slid it across her bigwig executive desk.

"Recognize the type there, Colonel? Take a good, hard look at it. Because your name is about to be emblazoned on the front page of the paper that made it famous. I'm not an ancient alien theorist asking for a pass to Roswell, ma'am. I'm an NYPD homicide cop working a homicide. You're the face of an organization that has just goofed up big-time. 'That's classified' isn't going to cut it. You guys need to get in front of this."

"Detective," she said with a stiff smile. "There are channels for this kind of thing that we have to abide by. Your request has been made. First, it has to be reviewed, and the information declassified after due process. Or feel free to try to get approval from the United States Foreign Intelligence Surveillance Court. Otherwise, I can't help you. Now, if you'll excuse me."

I looked at Emily. She seemed as pissed as I was. I couldn't believe this bull.

"One last question, Colonel. Do your superiors wind you up in the morning, or—like with drones—do they use WiFi control nowadays?" I said.

"Now, is that necessary, Detective? Please leave now or I'll have you escorted."

"Eardley was murdered," Emily said. "A pilot, a fellow airman, murdered. Thrown off a roof! You don't care about that, Colonel?"

"Of course I care," Payton said, maintaining a blank expression that said the exact opposite. "It's sad. I know lots of pilots, lots of dead ones, too. They get killed in combat. They commit suicide. Some of them get drunk and fall off buildings up in New York City after they go AWOL. Make sure to hand your security passes back when you get to the downstairs desk."

CHAPTER 15

"WELL, WE GAVE it a shot, at least. That's what really counts, right?" Emily said with mock cheeriness on the ride back to Union Station.

Even after she stopped the fed car, I sat there saying nothing. I looked out at the columned facade of the station, the people walking back and forth. When I spotted the wedding-cake white of the hovering Capitol dome off to the right, I felt like punching the dashboard.

"Washington is really something," I said. "It's one thing to not be able to find out something, quite another to be told it's being hidden from you on purpose—and don't let the door hit you in the ass."

"It's a disgrace," Emily said. "Did you contact Eardley's family yet?"

"No," I said. "That's one of the main reasons I came down here. Silly me. I thought I might find out what the hell happened so I'd have something to tell them. Imagine? Now I have to call this guy's mother and say, 'Good news, ma'am. Your son didn't die in a crash in '07, but, bad news, he died falling off a building last week. And no one in the military cares why.'"

"What really drives me crazy," Emily said, "is how stupid this is. The truth will come out eventually. These idiots can't see that?"

"They're bureaucrats, Emily," I said. "Bureaucrats by nature aren't the deepest of thinkers, or they wouldn't be bureaucrats. I'll tell you, the first thing I'm going to do after I contact Eardley's family is urge them to get a lawyer to sue the crap out of the Air Force and find out what the hell happened."

"You know what, Mike?" Emily said, drumming her fingers on the wheel. "Is it possible to hold off contacting the family one more day?"

"I guess I could ask the Medical Examiner to delay a little longer," I said. "But I want to get a move on so that Eardley's family can have a real burial. Why? What are you thinking?"

"That Air Force robo-witch was an ass, but Chris Milne truly is good people," Emily said. "Give him some time."

"Okay, Emily. I'll delay it a couple of days, but I won't hold my breath," I said, as she finally gave me a peck on the cheek good-bye.

CHAPTER 16

A MINUTE LATER I almost bumped into a handsome ponytailed college kid in jeans and a plaid shirt, playing the classical violin on the polished marble floor of the stunning Beaux Arts station.

Normally, positive things like classical music and grand architecture put a smile on my face, but I guess I wasn't in the mood. After my encounter with its power, the majestic polish of DC had really left a bad taste in my mouth. Like the robotic Air Force colonel's office, it was pleasant but seemed all veneer. Just something nice and distracting to look at while who-the-heck-knew-what went on behind the scenes.

My train wasn't due to leave for another half hour, so I decided to do some shopping. I was in the upper mezzanine level of the station in a cool old-fashioned general store called Union General, buying some gifts for the kids, when a woman bumped into me.

"Oh, I'm sorry," she said, reaching down and picking up a plastic bag off the floor. Gray-haired and middle-aged, she wore green nursing scrubs. "Here, sir. You dropped something."

"No, you're mistaken, ma'am. That's not mine," I said.

"You dropped this," she said again, and gave me a look. Then she turned and quickly left the store without looking back.

What the—? I stared after the woman as she disappeared into the crowd.

Inside the bag was a bottle of Coke and the *Washington Post*. Inside the *Post* was a folded piece of paper with a typed name and address.

Paul Haber
200 Lincoln Lane
Marble Spring, Pennsylvania

Under the name and address was a one-sentence message, also typed.

THIS MAN KNOWS WHAT YOU'RE LOOKING
FOR.

"How do you like that? Manna from heaven," I mumbled. I put the note back into the bag and headed quickly for the store exit.

CHAPTER 17

AN HOUR LATER, supplied with a huge coffee and a turkey sandwich from a DC deli, I was behind the wheel of a silver Chrysler 200 rental car. When I looked up Marble Spring on my phone and saw that it was only about four and a half hours from DC, I decided to find this guy, Haber, immediately—before the Air Force shut him up, too.

So I was riding up Interstate 270 through northern Maryland with no idea what I would find. A Google search of the name had yielded a frustrating lack of information, but a potential hit: one Paul Haber had been an Army platoon sergeant.

Okay, I was intrigued. But how had he found me? Did someone in DC tip him off? I thought back over the day—the security checkpoints at the Air Force base, the stonewalling at the Pentagon.

Had Payton had a change of heart? No way, I thought, remembering her expression after the phone call. She had too much to lose. Whoever was on the other end of that line wanted Eardley buried for good.

Chris Milne? No, he wouldn't bother with the cloak-and-dagger, the cryptic note.

My phone buzzed in the cup holder—Emily Parker. I picked up.

"It's been too long."

"Ha," she answered. "I'm guessing you're not on that train back to New York right now."

"And miss my date with Paul Haber?" I said. I'd texted her about the note, asking her if she could find anything on the mystery man.

"So I thought. Well, I have something interesting for you. I ran his name and he comes up clean in Army records, nothing unusual, spotless performance records—"

"And that's interesting?"

"So you don't want to know?"

"Know what?"

"That he served in Iraq, and his service overlapped with Eardley's. Both worked in special operations. And what's more, I also turned up a photo. Dated 2007."

Marble Spring was a blip on the map in rural Pennsylvania, up in the Allegheny Mountains. I now knew, thanks to Wikipedia, that it's four miles north of the west branch of the Susquehanna River, and has a population of 112. I practically have more people in my family.

I hooked a right on US 15 into Pennsylvania about an hour and twenty minutes later. Off the interstate, I got on State Route

PA 144, then crossed over onto PA 150 and started heading up into the Alleghenies. Stunning ridgeline views opened up as I crossed remote rusting bridges. Down in the distance was a patchwork of farms laid out along zigzagging rivers deep-cut into the heavily forested land.

It had stopped raining when I got out of DC, but around three o'clock it started to rain again. As I came down into a mountain valley alongside a railroad bed, thunder cracked what sounded like a foot from the car. The pelting rain began speed-drumming off the top of the Chrysler.

Five minutes later, I stopped before Marble Spring's single blinking yellow stoplight. Since there wasn't another driver to be seen, I paused to look around. Main Street, without even a bank or a post office, redefined the phrase "not much to look at." By my observation, the town consisted of a dollar store across from a Gothic-looking red brick church, and some sketchy-looking row houses rising up into the woods.

Behind these few structures, in fact all around them, stood the hills, dark and looming, the tops hidden in mist.

Still stopped at the light, I tried my email again. Service was spotty in the hills, but finally the photo from Emily had come through.

It showed our John Doe—Eardley—young and handsome in uniform. And looking very buddy-buddy with the guy next to him, who had an arm slung over Eardley's shoulder. Tall, also handsome, and apparently Paul Haber.

CHAPTER 18

I FOUND LINCOLN Lane about two miles west of the town. It was a narrow, steep strip of crumbling blacktop, more driveway than road. I counted three residences as I came up the long slope of the valley. Each was a trailerlike home set back under the trees, with old cars and jacked-up trucks in the front yards.

200 Lincoln Lane was the end of the road. I stopped the Chrysler and stared at the mailbox, which had the address but no name, and the dirt and gravel drive beside it curving still higher, back into the trees. You couldn't see any sign of the house.

The driveway was unbelievably long—three miles, if not more. You could hardly call it a driveway, since it wasn't paved. I thought I had made an idiotic mistake and was now driving on a state park hiking path. The Chrysler almost got stuck around a steep muddy curve but regained traction to make the top of the hill, where the road ended at a gate.

I stopped the car in front of it and saw that the gate was attached to a chain-link fence, with razor wire running along the top. There was a sign attached to the fence:

BLACK HILLS SECURITY INC.
Executive Training–AR-15 Proficiency–Survival Skills
Outdoor and Indoor Facilities
Corporate Weekends and Team Building
SKILLS TO LAST A LIFETIME!

Must be Haber's business, I thought. Through the wire, I could see the shooting range about half a football field away. It was very professional-looking, with covered shooting booths and macadam strips to shoot from one knee or prone, along with marked-off firing lanes. It seemed built for long-distance shooting, as the space between the booths and the gravel bullet stop—with hanging steel sheet targets—was immense.

Beside the range were wooden supply buildings and a raised range master booth. Off to the right, closer to the locked fence, I saw some small cabins, a storage container, and three new-looking double-wide trailers.

When I got out of the Chrysler I was greeted by a dog barking from inside the closest trailer—a vicious, rarely fed one by the sound of it.

Spotting a radio box next to the fence, I walked over and buzzed. There was no answer, and after a minute, I buzzed again.

Hmmm, I thought. No clients today, but there was the dog.

This Haber guy must have gone somewhere but might be back soon. So I decided to wait.

There were no bars on my phone or any WiFi signal. I looked at the GPS on the car. There was no town on the screen where my blip was. Not even the road registered. I was just a blip in the middle of nowhere.

CHAPTER 19

AFTER ABOUT AN hour, when the last vestiges of my sandwich and coffee were gone, I decided to head back to town to ask around at the store or the church for Haber.

I was almost to the part of the gravel drive where I'd thought I was on a hiking path when I saw the truck. It was a late-model red Nissan Titan pickup, sitting kind of cockeyed in the road with its front end tucked into the brush.

As I pulled closer, I could see a guy crouching by the Titan's rear driver's-side tire, working a lug wrench. His back was turned so I couldn't see his face, but he was short and stocky, wearing a camo ball cap and a black pullover hoodie and jeans.

"Hey, you okay?" I said, as I stopped the car, opened the Chrysler's door and got out. "You alright?"

"You move and I'll blow your spine out," said a voice off to my right.

I turned to my right and threw up my hands. Because on the hill a little ways up beside my car, a big dude in a balaclava and sunglasses was casually pointing a rifle at my head. The rifle was an FN SCAR, a smooth, almost plastic-looking beige Belgian machine gun with a suppressor on it. The gun's sight never moved an iota off my face as the big man easily hopped down onto the drive and came alongside my car.

Even with the gun pointed at me, I was actually more surprised than afraid. They were executives doing war game training or something, I decided. This was some kind of mistake.

"Whoa there, fellas. Everything's fine. I'm a friendly. I'm a cop, okay? You can put the gun down. I'm investigating a case. I'm looking for a guy who might know something about it. Paul's his name. Paul Haber. You know him?"

When I turned back toward the truck on my left, I saw the short guy suddenly right beside me. He was wearing a ski mask and sunglasses, too, and before I knew what was going on, he grabbed my shoulder and kicked my legs out from underneath me at the same time, and I landed hard enough on the gravel to knock the wind out of me.

Gasping for breath, I rolled to my right. My head banged off the hubcap of the Chrysler as I knelt up on all fours trying to get back on my feet. Then my Glock was ripped out of its holster as a big knee and a heavy weight landed on my neck like a sledgehammer, and I face-planted again back into the gravel.

I was stunned yet still trying to get up again when there was a familiar hollow clacking sound. My hands were ripped behind my back and a pair of handcuffs were ratcheted tight down on my wrists.

Still in shock, I heard an electronic beep.

"We just got him," the big guy said into a Motorola. "I repeat. He's under our control now. Over."

There was some radio chatter reply, but I couldn't hear what was being said. I was too busy lying there stunned as I felt my heart begin to double-time in my chest.

Just like that, in two seconds, I was out of it. Down and under the control of these two sons of bitches, out here in the middle of nowhere.

Just like that.

"Hey, you assholes, you better listen because I'm only going to tell you once," I said, after taking a long hard minute to regain the last scrap of my composure. "I don't know what you think you're doing, but I'm a cop. If you don't get these cuffs off me *right now,* you two are going to prison for felony assault on a law enforcement officer. That's ten years minimum."

"Ah, why don't we make it an even twenty, Officer," the short, stocky guy said as a Red Wing boot smashed into my chest.

"You want me to go for thirty or forty?" he said, kneeling down next to me as I fought for breath.

His voice right beside my ear was deep, hard as nails.

"Or do you want to shut the hell up?" he said.

I'm in trouble here, I thought as I stared up at the two hard, faceless men. I rolled over and lay gasping on the dirt road, staring out at the endless columns of trees.

Big, big trouble.

CHAPTER 20

THERE WAS SOME more chatter on the radio, and they put me into the truck, facedown on the floor between the rear seat and the front buckets. Shortie sat in the front with my Glock in his hand, while the big guy got behind the wheel, turned the truck over, and reversed it out of the ditch.

A fresh flood of fear rushed through me then as I suddenly realized who the big guy was. He was the guy who killed Eardley, who followed him up to the roof of the hotel and chucked him off.

They're going to kill me, too, I thought, as my fear began to morph into a full-on paralyzing terror.

I couldn't let that happen. To let that happen was to die, I knew. Training, training, you're trained. What to do in a situation like this? *Don't let your mind run away and hide on you,* I heard some long-ago instructor say like he was right there in the truck with me. Breathe, focus, and still yourself.

As we bumped along the dirt and gravel mountain road, I did just that. I took a breath and concentrated on just the air, and the way it felt coming in and out of my chest. After two or three breaths I actually felt much better—back to sheer panic instead of out-of-body terrified.

To keep myself from freaking out again, I forced myself to think.

I was still alive. Why? Why not just blow me away and bury me in the woods? Where the hell were they taking me?

They didn't know what to do with me, I realized; or I would already be dead. They needed to find out what I knew. Another blast of fear rocked through me. They were going to torture me to find out.

As I lay there with the horror of this new realization rattling through me, I suddenly found it. I figured out my one advantage, how they had screwed up. I had one window. It was tiny, almost microscopic, but I needed to take it. I had no other choice.

"*Ahhhhh!*" I suddenly screamed as we went over the next pothole. "My back! Ahhh! I have a bad back! The pain! I need to sit up!" I said, getting up on my knees.

"You do and I'll shoot you," Shortie said, putting the gun to my head.

"Do it, then, you son of a bitch! Shoot me!" I yelled as I continued to rise.

I heard him rack my gun.

"Fine, do it. Put me out of my fucking misery!" I screamed as I got up and sat on the seat.

And proceeded to go absolutely berserk.

I began by rearing back into the backseat and kicking Shortie right in his chin with the heel of my right shoe. Damn, that felt good. As he screamed in pain, I reared back again and kicked the big bastard of the driver hard in the back of his head with the heel of my other shoe.

Then I double-kicked out with my feet toward the windshield between the front bucket seats, jammed both of my feet into the steering wheel, and started thrashing around like the trapped animal that I was.

The big guy yelled as he hit the brakes, and the little guy was hitting me in the side of the head with the pistol butt, but then we were off the road in the woods, the truck went to the left sideways, and we were toppling over.

I'd never been in a rollover before. In the spinning cab, I bashed off the ceiling and the seats again and again like a sock in a dryer. The driver-side window smashed in and then the windshield. We kept rolling.

When we came to a stop, what felt like a million years later, we were right side up. Shortie's door was missing and so was Shortie. The roof on the right side had crumpled and come down about three feet. I looked to the left at the big dude, moaning, still belted in the driver's seat behind the deployed air bag.

I noticed his left arm had an open fracture, the bone protruding below his sleeve. As I stared at it, something warm flowed down the right side of my head and began dripping off my chin. I couldn't wipe at the blood because of the handcuffs.

I didn't know how I was still alive, and I didn't care. I wriggled away out the missing passenger-side door, dropped out of the crushed truck, and began to run into the woods.

CHAPTER 21

DEVINE WAITED IN the outer office of the comm trailer at Black Hills compound, listening to the boss, Paul Haber, scream bloody murder into his phone on the other side of the closed door.

He had reason to be pissed. They'd been only half an hour away, coming back from New York, when they got the call from Therkelson that the cop, Bennett, had arrived at the base alone.

Toporski and Therkelson, going ahead of the rest of the team, were supposed to neutralize the cop.

But that hadn't happened. As they came up the hill, they saw the wreckage in the ravine—Toporski squashed dead like a bug and his buddy Therkelson busted up and in critical condition. The cop was gone.

The only good news was that the cop seemed to have headed off in the direction of the state forest, hundreds of thousands of acres of uninhabited woods. He had a good forty-minute head start on them, but there was no one on this side of the mountain. They might be able to catch him still.

Haber had already gotten the hunting party started. Before

making the necessary calls, he told Monroe to get the MH-6 Little Bird ready, then took down and doled out what he called his M&M packs—M4A1s with attached M203 grenade launchers—to all the men.

Haber, who had been a platoon sergeant in the 2nd Battalion, 6th Infantry, before joining Delta, wasn't stingy with the ammo. He'd given everyone five full clips apiece, as well as grenade packs with star clusters and smoke and high-explosive rounds. He wanted this cop good and dead.

Devine sat on a plastic lawn chair staring up at the trailer's dull metal ceiling as Haber screamed some more.

Ever since he was a little boy, he'd loved guns and hunting and the woods. His father was an avid deer hunter, as his father had been before him. Devine loved the cold, empty wilderness and the smell of gun oil and cordite, sweat, and leather.

But for the first time, he felt something was wrong about all this, something off.

There were only seven of them now. Haber, Irvine, Leighton, Willard, Monroe, and De Souza. And himself.

One little, two little, three little Indians, Devine thought as the boss's door flew open.

CHAPTER 22

HABER STOOD IN the doorway, a slender, sharp-featured thirty-five-year-old man with a shaved head, gray trimmed goatee, and cold, dark-brown eyes. He was dressed in Sitka Optifade camo bibs and jacket, with Crispi Italian hunting boots. The mission was bankrolled by some deep pockets, and Haber had insisted that he and the men be outfitted properly with the best that money could buy.

Even at rest, Haber had a stately presence. There was something old-fashioned about him. A hunter, an alpha. A born leader.

"Get in here," Haber said, going back into the office, taking his own M&M pack out of the locker behind him and clunking it on his desk.

Devine watched Haber expertly load, check, and sight his automatic weapon. He did it with a skilled workman's quick yet reverent efficiency. There was something pretty about it. Like watching a musician tuning his instrument, or a master chef honing his knife.

The inside of his office was as spare and rugged as the man. A cot and camp chair, coffeepot on a plywood shelf, a whiteboard tacked with aerial and topographical maps.

"Where's Leighton? Here?" Haber said, tapping at the map.

"Yes. I have him on this perimeter," Devine said, stepping over and drawing a line with his finger.

"So you definitely think he went south here?" Haber said, pointing.

"Yes. His track through the mud puts him on this downslope to the southwest right toward the state land. That's our advantage. That's some of the most uninhabited timberland in the state. In the northeast, probably."

"Okay, good," Haber said. "Why aren't you on the bird yet?"

Devine winced.

"I wanted to talk to you in private, sir. I think we should medevac out Therkelson. We could have Monroe fly him over the hill and down to Chapman and call 911 anonymously."

"C'mon, he has a broken arm," Haber said. "Last thing we need is more heat."

"I think his back is broke, too, sir."

Haber glanced at him angrily.

"He's stabilized, right?"

"But there could be internal bleeding."

"Don't give me 'could be,' Devine. Don't be an old biddy. Therk is old-school tough. Just give him some morphine until we get this thing settled. Then we'll get him completely patched up."

"You sure, boss?"

Haber glared at him. Not a comfortable feeling. Yet he went on.

"I mean, maybe we should retreat, sir. Get out of here. Re-assess. We're starting to take some serious casualties now. We're down to seven guys."

"Not that I need to explain this to you, Devine, but I just got off the phone with our southern friends who are bankrolling the operation, and we've agreed to ramp up the schedule. We leave tomorrow. They'll have good men at the airfield to replace the ones we lost. It's all set up."

"Tomorrow we go?"

"Yes, buddy, and we're leaving here right away. After we bag the cop, we're scrubbing this entire hill. Gone without a trace. Is that good enough for you, you worrywart?"

Haber smiled then as he pounded Devine in the arm.

Devine smiled back.

O Captain, my Captain, he thought.

"Sir, yes, sir," he said.

CHAPTER 23

BUMPING AND TRIPPING, sweating and bleeding, with my arms still handcuffed behind my back, I ran down the endless slope of the middle-of-nowhere Pennsylvania forest.

Crossing a narrow creek, I slipped and did another long roll that ended in a full somersault before I came to a painful, skidding stop in the wet forest leaves.

As I lay there spitting dirt out of my mouth, a memory surfaced from when I was a kid—when we'd play army in the woods of Van Cortlandt Park in the Bronx, using sticks that looked like rifles as we patrolled. I fought back a desperate urge to start weeping.

Instead, I stood and continued southwest. I would have headed back toward the road I'd taken there, except I had no idea where I was in this damned woodland maze. I knew west by the hastily setting sun, but what the hell did that gain me? Which way was help?

The one thing I could do was pick a direction—southwest— and keep steadily moving to distance myself from the wrecked truck. Because whoever was on the other end of that big dude's phone would be coming after me, and they were going to be pissed. I still didn't know a damn thing except that these guys were killers, of the professional CIA-military variety; and I now, like a complete idiot, was in their home court.

After another quarter-mile, I came to a small cliff—three or four stories of angled gray rock. I could have run down it if my arms were at my sides, but I couldn't risk tripping, so I had to inch down like an infant.

At the bottom, I looked to the left and saw something sparkle through the brush. It was a creek, I saw. I walked over to it. A stream heading the same way I was, southwest. It was wider than the one I'd tripped over; and running water would lead to more, bigger running water, wouldn't it? That might mean fishermen, a boat, perhaps a bridge.

But as I followed the stream down, it began to slow. When I came to the foot of the wooded hill, I saw that it became a trickle that fed an enormous wetland swamp. "There goes my merit badge," I mumbled. I went to the left, following the curve of the wide hill.

I was at the edge of the swamp, where it seemed to become dry land again, when I began to hear it. To the left beside the swamp was a stand of tall, very skinny white trees with yellow leaves, and a lot of brush; and from the brush came the faint sound of chirping.

At first I thought it was a bunch of birds, but it was too

consistent. It sounded mechanical. A weird kind of electronic beeping, like a smoke alarm or a truck backing up, which made zero sense.

I thought I was cracking up when I heard a dog bark from the same direction. Initially it sounded like the beast I'd heard from the trailer—but it was a friendlier bark.

"Help! Help me, please! Hello?" I yelled, running for the brush and the white trees.

I was about twenty feet into the stand, crashing through the brush, when through the tangle of vines and twigs I saw Day-Glo orange.

A moment later I recognized the bright orange color as two hunting vests—and hope leapt in my heart in a way I had never felt.

CHAPTER 24

THEY WERE GROUSE hunters. Joe Walke, a tall, heavyset, bearded man with glasses, and his granddaughter Rosalind, who looked no older than fourteen.

The beeping came from the pointing collar of their English setter, Roxie, a floppy pooch with brown, black, and white fur. Roxie would be let off the leash into the woods to find the grouse and, when she did, would assume a pointing position—triggering the electronic beeping of the collar.

But I learned that later. When I first saw the older man and his granddaughter, they were pointing shotguns at me as I burst out of the bush, handcuffed and covered in filth and blood.

"Please help me! A bunch of men are trying to kill me!" I yelled.

While I panted in terror, trying to speak, Mr. Walke lowered the gun and came over. He calmly sat me down and washed out my head cut with a bottle of water from his pack.

"It's okay, son. Slowly now. What's really going on? Are you a fugitive of some sort? Why are you wearing handcuffs?"

I shook my head at him violently.

"There's no time. A phone. Do you have a phone?"

"She has one, but I make her leave it back at the vehicle. Breaks her concentration," Walke said, smiling.

He had a good and gentle whiskered face.

"Wouldn't work, anyway. Not out here. No bars," said Rosalind, a scrawny tomboyish girl with short, sandy hair and freckles.

"I'm a police officer," I finally managed to get out. "From New York City. I was just attacked by two men up at that shooting range on top of the mountain who I was trying to question. I managed to escape, but they have friends who are right this very second trying to find me. If they do, they will kill me and you. These guys are soldiers, professional killers. We need to leave this place now."

"Don't believe him, Grandpa. He's lying," Rosalind said, shaking her head. "Leave him. He's a bad man. Let's just get out of here and call the cops."

"At that shooting range, huh?" Walke said, nodding as he looked back up the hill. "I knew those fellas seemed fishy."

"You don't believe him, Grandpa, do you?" Rosalind said.

"Yes, I do," Walke said, helping me up. "Let's get back to the ATVs."

I sat in front of Walke on his Honda ATV, cradled in his arms like a baby in a basket, as we skirted the swampland back to the pickup he had parked four miles away.

As the woods flew away behind us, I couldn't stop thinking about how lucky I was. About God answering my prayers. When we arrived at the blue truck and Mr. Walke cut the chain of the cuffs with a pair of side cutters he took from the toolbox, I was seriously thinking about hugging him.

We'd gotten both ATVs back into the bed of the truck and had just started the engine when we heard it. It was a distant sound, almost pleasant at first like a lawn mower, but then we could hear its trilling. It was a helicopter, flying low and fast over the swamp.

"That them?" Mr. Walke said.

I nodded.

"Let's get the hell out of here."

"Grandpa, what have you gotten us into now? Grandma is gonna kill you," Rosalind said, sitting beside me with Roxie in her lap.

Joe Walke dropped the truck into drive and dropped the hammer.

"What else is new, child?" he said, as we bumped and skidded off down the old dirt logging road.

CHAPTER 25

THE WHIZZING ROTORS of the black MH-6 chopper that Haber called the Black Egg of Death slammed at the air above as they followed the slope of the hill down. Like a skier coasting down a ramp, the wasplike aircraft floated down the ridge low enough to put stars on the tops of the hemlocks and white pines it skimmed.

As in Iraq, Paul Haber sat in the skid seat of the helicopter poised like a bronco-busting cowboy in the chute. He had aviator sunglasses perched atop his head and the butt of the M4A1 held jauntily off his hip, right hand in front of the trigger guard, in a textbook field-manual ready position.

Devine knew that the real authority of military men and leaders lies in the half-magical, half-insane ability to lead by example, to dive headlong into combat with calm and confidence. How many times had he seen Haber expose himself to devastating fire without hesitation?

Haber could do anything, Devine thought, his doubts and fears long gone. Haber wasn't like regular men.

As in Iraq, when Haber was his hero, Devine watched closely

what he did, how his hunter's eyes tracked into the boughs of the endless trees.

"Sir, three o'clock," said Willard, on the aircraft's other side.

The bird swung to the right. On Sweetheart Mountain, the opposite hill of the river valley beyond the swamp, there was movement up an old logging road. It was a faded blue pickup. Dirt spat out from the rear tires as it struggled up the steep grade.

"Is it him?" Haber called over the intercom.

"I can't tell," Devine said, trying to make out anyone in the cab. It was practically impossible with the vibration of the chopper.

Haber grabbed the glasses and looked himself.

"It has to be. Get after the truck."

The chopper's nose tilted downward and they sped forward over the swamp. Reaching the opposite side, they could see the blue pickup make the top of the hill. Instead of continuing on the logging road down the other side, the truck lurched to the left and continued along the top of an exposed rocky ridge, bouncing up and down off the bumpy rock face crazily as it picked up speed.

"What the hell is it doing?" Devine said.

"Who cares? Get up on that damned ridge and give me a clear shot."

They'd just reached the top of the ridge, coming up behind the truck, when it happened. The driver's-side door of the speeding truck opened and a man slid out, tumbling, skidding, and kicking up a cloud of rocks and dust. Into the air on the other side of the ridge, like Evel Knievel trying to jump the Grand Canyon, the still-speeding driverless truck sailed straight off the other side of the cliff and disappeared nose-first from view.

"What the—?" Haber said, and laughed. "Get me down there! Get me down there now!" The helicopter touched down in the tight clearing at the top of the ridge, where the truck's driver had landed and was still sitting. As they jumped out and approached, Devine saw he was an old man, dressed in an orange vest and waders.

"Who the hell are you?" Haber said to him.

"I'm Joe Walke," he said. He held his glasses in both hands and looked over the cliff, where the truck had shattered against the boulders far down below. "It wasn't my fault. He wouldn't jump. I told him."

"Who wouldn't jump?"

"That New York cop you're chasing," Walke said. "I thought we could bail and shake you, but he didn't get my gist, I guess."

"That cop is down there in the truck?"

Walke nodded.

"Poor fella," he said.

Devine stood over the old coot, while Haber sent Irvine and Leighton down in the chopper to check out the truck.

"There's nobody in there," Irvine radioed up after another three minutes. "The old fart's lying."

"What?" the old man said, looking down at the truck again.

"No? That's funny. I could have sworn I seen him right there next to me. He must have jumped after all."

Haber looked out down the ridge, the thin silver filament of the river in the shadowed land in the distance. It was past sunset now, getting dark.

"I wanted to wrap this up before dark, but now that won't happen, will it?" Haber said, and hit the old man square in his face with the rifle butt.

The old man turned with the blow. Then he turned back and spat out a tooth.

"You think you're tough, hitting an old man? You ain't shit."

"And you're what?" Haber said as he leaned down over him. "Mr. Shit, I presume?"

The old man rolled up his sleeve and showed him a tattoo on his bicep, green and smeary with age. Devine recognized it. It was the skull and wings of force recon. USMC '68, it said beneath it.

"That's who I am. Right there. *Semper fi,* you asshole."

CHAPTER 26

THREE HOURS LATER, we came upon the sign between two stone posts. It was metal, in the shape of an arrow, lying rusted on the ground beneath a cracked wood beam.

Big Country Secret Cavern, it read, in Jet Age 1950s script.

It was Joe Walke's idea. If he wasn't convinced by my story, he knew we were in danger when he spotted the man with the gun riding on the outside of the helicopter.

There was no way to drive out of the area without being spotted from the air, so Joe insisted we bail while he drew Haber and his men off in another direction. A former coal miner and also the son of a coal miner, he'd spent his whole life in the area and could navigate the woods blindfolded. Rosalind, too, knew a special way out on foot.

"This place was big a long time ago, but it's been closed for years. Even the road is gone," Rosalind said as we stepped past the sign, Roxie at our heels.

In the low moonlight, I saw that there was an indentation in the hill we'd been skirting. It was just rock face along this side, ten stories of it going straight up.

Twenty feet later, we saw the cave opening. It was triangular, like a church roof, and it was on the other side of a huge black pond.

"How are we going to get through? Swim? It's filled with water."

"No, this way," Rosalind said, going left around the oblong pond. "They used to send you through in paddle boats, Tunnel of Love–style, Grandpa said, but there's a walkway. C'mon."

As we stepped in under the cathedral-like ceiling, Roxie started barking.

"Stop your fidgeting, Roxie. I like it as much as you do."

I turned on one of the flashlights Joe Walke had given us. We also had some water bottles, and the shotguns—they held about twenty rounds, most of them number 7 birdshot, but there were a few shells of double-ought buck.

What wasn't in our favor was that the shotguns were over-and-under break-open style, so they could only hold two rounds at a time. If we got into a firefight with these professional military folks, it was going to be over very quickly.

The beam of the flashlight revealed some beer bottles and graffiti on the rough rock wall, but they looked old and faded. I pointed the flashlight down the cement lip of the path beside the canal-like waterway. The path continued for at least a foot-ball field and then seemed to disappear to the right.

"You sure the other side isn't blocked or anything?" I asked.

"No way. The other side is even more open than this one. It would take an earthquake," Rosalind said.

We walked deeper into the eerie, dead-silent cave. The rough rock walls had a lunar quality, seeming to shift as the light moved over them. Some sections had weird patterns and folds. Embedded minerals in other areas glittered and threw back the light in disco-ball constellations.

Even on a day when I'd had a gun to my head, in this claustrophobic space my nerves ached to turn around. It was like we'd just walked in through the gates of hell.

"Marshall, Will, and Holly, on a routine expedition," I sang, as I pointed the light up at cone-shaped rock stalagmites—or were they stalactites? It had been a while since I'd been underground, in the middle of nowhere, in the middle of the night.

"What's that?" Rosalind asked.

"From a show I used to watch when I was your age called *Land of the Lost*. Ever hear of it?" I asked.

"No," she said, leading onward into the dark. "We don't have a TV. Grandpa says TV makes people stupid."

"He may be onto something there," I said. What a brave and capable little girl.

We finally reached the opening. When we stepped into the glorious open air from the long and nightmarish tunnel, I saw that the canal led into a huge lake. We were on the other side of the hill now. We'd walked straight through the mountain.

I looked back. The roof of the tunnel was an almost perfectly rectangular slab of rock about ten feet thick. It looked like a knocked-over monolith, like the roof of Stonehenge half-buried in the earth.

"People actually paid to do that?" I said.

"So I'm told," Rosalind said, shaking her head.

"How long is it to this town? What's it called?"

"Chapman. About eight miles around the other side of this lake."

"Wait! Get down!" I said. "I see something."

About a mile away, along the left shore of the lake, there was a light. A flashlight. Somebody walking, coming toward us. Worse than that, I thought I heard a short bark.

"You gotta be kidding me," I mumbled. *What are we going to do now?*

I looked back at the mouth of the cavern, then toward the slope of the hill above it. It was steep, filled with trees, but manageable.

"But that heads right back up the hill to their camp," Rosalind whispered. "Don't we want to go away from there?"

"We have no choice. C'mon," I whispered, and slung the shotgun over my shoulder.

CHAPTER 27

DAWN WAS BREAKING as we topped the crest of the ridge.

The whole top of the mountain was covered in a silver mist that turned to a spectacular rose-gold in the light of the rising sun. If I wasn't being hunted down like a rabbit by a group of what had to be Special Forces soldiers, I bet I would have appreciated it even more.

Rosalind and I were freezing and exhausted. We'd only slept a little the night before, forty-five-minute catnaps in two different spots up the hill. We'd heard the helicopter twice, but it hadn't sounded very close, thankfully.

There wasn't a peep out of Rosalind or Roxie during the climb. I couldn't believe what a great dog that setter was. She, too, knew we were in very deep trouble.

We had been walking down a small wooded rise for about twenty minutes when the mist started to lift. You could actually see the moisture rising slowly, like a stage curtain showing the feet of the trees.

And then a few seconds later, we stopped when we suddenly saw something.

Ahead of us about a hundred feet away, there was a man sitting on the ground, his back turned, leaning against a blown-over tree.

CHAPTER 28

THOUGH SEATED, HE appeared tall and lanky, wearing camo, a gun propped on the log next to him.

Gripping our cold shotguns, we knelt on the forest floor and watched him for a very long and silent five minutes.

He didn't move. Was he sleeping? Dead? Or was it a trap?

Very slowly I began walking down toward him. When I was about ten feet away, the guy sort of stirred and reached for his weapon.

I closed the gap and put both barrels of the shotgun to the back of his head. "Don't!" I said.

I made him lie on his belly, searched his outer pockets, and found zip ties that I used on his hands. Twenty feet away from where he'd been sleeping, the trees gave way to a clearing I recognized as the firing range I'd seen the day before. Beyond it were the trailers.

We'd done it. We'd made it back to their camp. I told Rosalind to head to the tree line and wait for me there, while I went back to the soldier and lifted his weapon—an actual grenade launcher! Just amazing. These guys had to be CIA or something. You couldn't get grenade launchers at Walmart. I'd never even seen one.

The man remained silent as I removed his camo balaclava. He looked boyish, in his late thirties, a pleasant enough curly-haired guy with a goofy gap in his teeth. His driver's license said his name was Justin De Souza, with an address in San Jose, California.

"Long way from San Jose, Justin," I said. I found a Clif energy bar in his bag, ripped off the wrapper, and started chewing.

"Where are the others?" I said, spitting crumbs.

"Where the hell do you think they are? Out looking for you."

"You're the only one here?" I said skeptically.

"Yes. I mean no. Therkelson is in the trailer with a broken back. And the old man is here. They got him locked up."

"The old guy in the blue truck? He's here?"

"Yes. He's okay. A little roughed up, but okay."

"Get up and show me," I said, kicking him.

We walked to the clearing and stopped.

"Rosalind, I'm going to take this guy back over to those trailers. If something happens, I want you and Roxie to try to get to Chapman by yourself. But if it's okay, I'll whistle and you and Roxie run as fast as you can to the trailers, okay?"

"Okay," she said. "Where's my grandpa?"

"In one of the trailers, I think. Just let me go check first."

I turned back to Justin.

"Okay, buddy. Showtime. If you're lying and somebody takes a shot at me, I won't shoot back at him. I will pull this trigger on you, Justin, and we can die together. Now get moving. Fast."

The twenty seconds it took to run out in the open toward the trailers were the longest of my life. Any moment, I thought I would know what it felt like to take a high-powered bullet to a vital part of my body. But we made it. There were no shots.

We found Joe Walke in the second trailer, sitting against the wall in his orange vest.

"You got the drop on them!" he said, leaping up with surprising energy. "I knew it! Where's Rosalind?"

I whistled.

Their hug moments later on the edge of the firing range was epic. Roxie, who couldn't contain herself any longer, let out a happy bark.

"Okay, Joe. Here's what I'd like you to do. Find some keys, take one of the vehicles, and head down the hill."

"What are you going to do?"

"My job," I said, shoving Justin back into the trailer in front of me, "is to end this thing. Now go."

CHAPTER 29

I MADE JUSTIN sit against the wall.

"You ever want to make it back to San Jose in the vertical position, you better start explaining just what in the hell is going on here, Justin. Because I've had a long night, and I'm not in the mood."

"We're training at the camp."

"Training for what? The coming alien invasion? I'm a cop, Justin. NYPD. I know what happened to Eardley. How he didn't die in the crash back in '07. How his old buddy Haber is here running a paramilitary operation, and decided Eardley should take a dive off the side of a building. What are you guys? CIA?"

Justin looked at me.

I took a chance. "Look, man. I have no stake in this, except that I tried to solve a murder and now people keep shooting at me. But I was just at the Pentagon, asking how this guy turned up dead again, and the brass are all over this. The secret is out."

Justin grunted, so I continued. "And this little training camp is gonna look pretty strange when the powers that be start sniffing around. I wouldn't be surprised if Haber took that chopper and flew away. If not, I'm gonna wait here with your weapon to greet him in style. But if you tell me what's going on, I can help you."

He exhaled and slumped down. "Give me a cigarette, man. They're in my bag. I'll tell you the whole thing. This mission is cursed."

I lit his Marlboro for him with his Zippo and placed it between his lips.

"Okay, Justin. Now, from the very beginning," I said.

He took a breath.

"It all started in Iraq. On the night of May 1, 2007, we ran a raid from the Special Forces command in Balad up north all the way down south. Near the shore of the Persian Gulf in Basra."

"In Eardley's C-130?"

"Yeah. It was a big CIA-run operation. There were Rangers, Green Berets, and SEALs. I was just a weatherman and forward observer."

"Weatherman?"

"An Air Force weatherman. They bring us out on potentially longer raids to read the sky, just like the guys on Channel 6. Weather's important to pilots and planes. Like life-and-death important."

I nodded.

"Go on."

"Anyway, so the top special operators, mostly veteran SEALs, were real jazzed about grabbing some bigwig al-Qaeda asshole they got intel on, so they brought all the toys way down there. Little bird choppers, some Humvees, some dirt bikes. There were about thirty of us altogether.

"So the hot dogs do a recon, to suss out a plan while a contingent of Rangers and B-level folks like myself are supposed to hang back at this remote staging area, as backup in case some heavy-duty shit goes down. While all the hotshots were on surveillance for hours, us peewees were sitting around shooting the shit. And this one Ranger, this guy Toporski, goes exploring on the outskirts of this remote craphole suburb of Basra. After an hour, he radioes us to come running because somebody took a shot at him.

"We run over there, and there's another shot from this hut's window, and we light it up and kick in the door ready to grease Osama, who we hadn't found yet. But it was better than that. A million times better. It was the mother lode."

CHAPTER 30

I STILL HADN'T heard the chopper coming back but knew it could return at any second. I nudged Justin to keep him talking.

"Back in 2003 when we came in, the week before we got to Baghdad, a national bank was knocked over by the guards who were supposed to watch it. Three hundred million in cash and gold. Well, I don't know how that loot got there to Basra in some shithole of a hut, but that's where it was."

I couldn't believe what I was hearing. Treasure hunting in Basra?

"There it was in a locked room under a tarp. There were two pallets. On one was millions of dollars in Federal Reserve US hundred-dollar bills, and on the other pallet were stacks of gold bars up to the waist. There were 105 of them in all. Each one twenty-seven pounds of pure gold, with the word *Engelhard* stamped into them. I've seen a few things, but when Toporski pulled that tarp, that took the cake. I mean, it was just...

"Right then and there, we decide to take it. Don't tell the hotshots. Screw them. All six of us—including Haber and Eardley, our pilot—grab it all, load it into the Humvee. We had to take out the seats. The truck was scraping the ground. Then we hauled ass back to the plane."

"And did what with it? How would you get it out of the country?"

"Eardley comes up with a plan. He's gonna drop this gold- and money-filled Humvee from the plane into this lake he knows up north near the base, just open the back ramp and put it in neutral and dump her out. Mark its location, and we're going to come back and get it."

"Like sunken treasure."

"Exactly, man. Like pirate booty. Then he's gonna crash the plane, fake his death, and get out of the country."

"Nobody stopped him?"

"No way. He was on a desert landing strip. Not like he had to ask the tower for permission. It was war."

"What did you say when the others got back? Didn't they ask where Eardley and the plane went?"

"What do you think we said? We don't know. Acted like he just went nuts or something."

"And they bought it?"

"Yep. Didn't find a body, but with the plane down—they shut the case."

"So how did he get out of Iraq?"

"He said he put a good chunk of money in a knapsack before dumping the rest in the lake, and found a guy in a pickup to drive him to the border. He bought a fake passport. He was a smart guy. He learned some Arabic. He would joke around with the Iraqis. He was a likable guy, with giant balls. I miss him."

"Bullshit," I said. "You killed him."

"Not me. That was that asshole Therkelson. He said it was an accident."

"So what's all this here?" I said. "The camp and everything."

Justin smiled.

"You're going back for the rest of the money!"

He nodded.

"Exactly. We were training to go back into Iraq to snatch it. It's in ISIS-held territory now."

"But at the last second, Eardley bugged out," I said, thinking about his reaching out to the reporter.

"I guess. He wasn't the same after. He and Haber used to be buddies, you know. We all were. And we looked up to those two. Would have followed wherever they led. But Haber took over the training operation and brought in some…investors. The stakes got higher."

"And Eardley had regrets?"

"I mean, he'd made this split-second decision to fake his death…he traveled the world, but he wanted his life back. The money wasn't worth living the rest of his days underground, a war criminal instead of a hero. So he disappeared. Which we knew meant he was gonna blow the whistle on us all. Except the boss man tracked him down. Got to him before he could betray us."

"And here we are."

"And here we are," Justin repeated, as the trill of the helicopter sounded out the open door behind us.

CHAPTER 31

I LOOKED OUT the door and saw the little black bird come down out of the sky directly above the firing range, silver tatters of mist trailing behind like a wedding gown's train.

Then the guns on the helicopter's underbelly opened. Wide.

I dove to the plywood ground of the trailer as Justin lunged out the door.

I pressed myself into the corner as the chopper's minigun tore the trailer in half. The sound of it was industrial, the scream of a table saw ripping a two-by-four. The floor I was hugging shook as if caught in a tornado, a violent storm of lead and tracers that tore the roof off the structure like a can opener.

I was still shaking, my deafened ears ringing, when the two guys grabbed me and dragged me out of the smoking, burned metal ruins of the trailer. Out onto the cool grass of the range I was dragged and dropped.

A hunting boot hit me in the face, the little metal lace hooks opening my lip like a razor.

"That's for killing my friend, you son of a bitch," I heard one of the three camo-clad bozos say through the ringing of my ears. "And crippling the other one. He'll never walk again because of what you did."

"My pleasure," I yelled as I thumbed at my lip. "Anytime."

"Hey," Justin said, looking around. "The girl and the old man. Where the hell did they go?"

"Girl?"

"Yeah, the damn girl who was with him. She has a gun."

"We'll find her in a second," said the slimmest of them.

"You must be Paul Haber," I said. "The leader of this band of merry asswipes."

"Now, now, Detective. I have a mission to run, and chasing you all the hell around these mountains has been quite a delay. Good-bye now. You can shoot him, Devine, any time you're ready. We need to get going."

CHAPTER 32

THAT'S WHEN I came out and said it.

"Your coordinates are wrong," I said calmly. "I have them."

"What?" Haber said, turning back to me.

"Eardley had them in his stomach. In a condom. Twenty-four numbers. He must have known you guys were close, so he swallowed them. You don't have the right ones. I do."

"You're bluffing."

"Am I?" I said, forcing a laugh. "Fine. Go over there and get your head chopped off for nothing."

"You gotta be shitting me, boss," said the guy who had kicked me. "This mission is doomed, sir. I told you."

"This mission is not doomed," Haber said, as a high-pitched beep came through on their radios.

"Come in, you dummies. Dummies, come in. Over."

I smiled. It was Rosalind.

"What the—?" Haber said.

"Listen up. My grandpa's got your friend's gun, and he's got a bead on your head, mister. Now drop your gun or he'll blast your head off."

The sound of the silenced bullet that hit Haber's head as he swung up with his rifle for the tree line beyond the range was insignificant, but what it did to his head was very significant. Half headless, he toppled over backward as if it were a trust team-building exercise. Not surprisingly, no one caught him.

"Now my grandpa's got the bead on you other guys," the girl's voice said over the radio. "Drop your guns if you don't want to get shot, too."

They dropped their guns.

I stood and picked one up.

"Mr. Walke, I thought I told you to leave," I said into Haber's radio, as I saw the good old man emerge from the trees with his granddaughter and dog.

"Yeah, well, I don't hear so well sometimes," he radioed back.

EPILOGUE

IT WAS ABOUT two hours later when I drove my rental Chrysler 200 back down the mountain, around the line of the Pennsylvania State Trooper cars.

Joe Walke sat beside me, and Rosalind and Roxie slept in the back.

"I owe you my life, both of you," I said to Mr. Walke, as we pulled up in front of a crumbling old Victorian in Marble Spring, a block behind the church.

"You're good people, Mike. You would have done no different for us, were we in trouble. Good people are the same everywhere. They help each other."

"They tuned you up pretty good, and you lost your truck and the ATVs. I feel terrible."

"Ah, the vehicles are insured, and a crack or two to this old noggin ain't nothing at all. I actually feel sorry for those stupid young men."

"Sorry for them?"

"Look what we as a nation asked them to do. Go off to war,

ride on helicopters, and kill people in some far-off hellhole. Then they come back, and we ignore them. Too busy playing with our phones. We couldn't care less.

"Any wonder these kids would want to line their own pockets? Hell, everybody else seems to be doing the same thing these days."

"Not everybody," I said, and shook his hand.

"So long, Mike," Mr. Walke said with a wink. He lifted his sleeping granddaughter out of the backseat. "You find yourself around these parts again, look me up. We'll go down to the veterans' hall for a jar or two."

"Will do," I said, smiling.

He'd just closed the rear door of the car when my phone, sitting there in the drink holder, started to ring. I'd glanced at it coming into town and had seen the screen filled with messages.

"Hello. Mike here," I said.

"Sweet mother of hope, you're alive," Mary Catherine said. "Well, thanks for calling, Mike. We haven't been worried sick about you or anything. What happened, the case went late? You decided to stay over in DC? That Parker woman wasn't around, was she? You better hope not."

"I stayed over in Pennsylvania, actually," I said.

"Pennsylvania?"

"Well, it's sort of a long story," I said, glancing back up at the misty hills above the town as I followed the state road toward home.

"DON'T MAKE A SOUND. NOT A SINGLE SOUND."

Someone is luring men from the streets to play a mysterious, high-stakes game in the English countryside. Former Special Forces officer David Shelley will go undercover to shut it down. But this might be a game he can't win.

The hunt is on.

Read on for a special excerpt from the shocking new thriller
Hunted, **coming soon from**

BOOK**SHOTS**

TWO MEN TROD carefully through the trees in search of their prey. Bluebells and wild garlic were underfoot, beech and Douglas firs on all sides, tendrils of early morning fog still clinging to the damp slopes. Somewhere in this wood was the quarry.

The man in front, feeling brave thanks to the morning sherry, his bolt-action Purdey and the security man covering his back, was Lord Oakleigh. A Queen's Counsel lawyer of impeccable education, he had an impressive listing in *Debrett's* and his peer's robes were tailored by Ede & Ravenscroft. Oakleigh had long ago decided that these accomplishments paled in comparison to the way he felt now—this particular mix of adrenaline and fear, this feeling of being so close to death.

This, he had decided, was life. And he was going to live it.

The car had collected him at 4:00 a.m. He'd taken the eye mask he was given, relaxed in the back of the Bentley, and used the opportunity for sleep. In a couple of hours he arrived at the estate. He recognized some of his fellow hunters, but not all—there were a couple of Americans and a Japanese gentleman he'd never seen before. Nods were exchanged. Curtis and Boyd of The Quarry Co. made brief introductions. All weapons were checked to ensure they were smart-modified, then they were networked and synced to a central hub.

The tweed-wearing English contingent watched, bemused, as the Japanese gentleman's valet helped him into what looked like tailored disruptive-pattern clothing. Meanwhile the shoot security admired the TrackingPoint precision-guided rifle he carried. Like women fussing over a new baby, they all wanted a hold.

As hunt time approached, the players fell silent. Technicians wearing headphones unloaded observation drones from an operations van. Sherry on silver platters was brought around by blank-faced men in tailcoats. Curtis and Boyd toasted the hunters and, in his absence, the quarry. Lastly, players were assigned their security—Oakleigh was given Alan, his regular man—before a distant report indicated that the hunt had begun and the players moved off along the lawns to the treeline, bristling with weaponry and quivering with expectation.

Now deep in the wood, Oakleigh heard the distant chug of Land Rover engines and quad bikes drift in on a light breeze. From overhead came the occasional buzz of a drone, but otherwise it was mostly silent, even more so the further into the wood they ventured and the more dense it became. It was just the way he liked it. Just him and his prey.

"Ahead, sir," came Alan's voice, urgent enough that Oakleigh dropped to one knee and brought the Purdey to his shoulder in one slightly panicked movement. The wood loomed large in his cross hairs, the undergrowth keeping secrets.

"Nothing visible," he called back over his shoulder, then cleared his throat and tried again, this time with less shaking in his voice. "Nothing up ahead."

"Just hold it there a moment or so, sir, if you would," replied Alan, and Oakleigh heard him drop his assault rifle to its strap and reach for his walkie-talkie. "This is red team. Request status report…"

"Anything, Alan?" Oakleigh asked over his shoulder.

"No, sir. No visuals from the drones. None of the players report any activity."

"Then our boy is still hiding."

"It would seem that way, sir."

"Why is he not trying to make his way to the perimeter? That's what they usually do."

"The first rule of combat is to do the opposite of what the enemy expects, sir."

"But this isn't combat. This is a hunt."

"Yes, sir."

"And it isn't much of a hunt if the quarry's hiding, is it?" Oakleigh heard the note of indignation in his voice and knew it sounded less like genuine outrage and more like fear, so he put his eye back to the scope and swept the rifle barrel from left to right, trying to keep a lid on his nerves. He wanted a challenge. But he didn't want to die.

Don't be stupid. You're not going to die.

But then came the crackle of distant gunfire, quickly followed by a squall of static.

"Quarry spotted. Repeat: quarry spotted."

Oakleigh's heart jackhammered and he found himself in two minds. On the one hand, he wanted to be in the thick of the action. Last night he'd even entertained thoughts of being the winning player, imagining the admiration of his fellow hunters, ripples that would extend outwards to London and the corridors of power, the private members' clubs of the Strand, and chambers of Parliament.

On the other hand, now that the quarry had shown himself capable of evading the hunters and drones for so long, he felt differently.

From behind came a rustling sound and then a thump. Alan made a gurgling sound.

Oakleigh realized too late that something was wrong and wheeled around, fumbling with the rifle.

A shot rang out and Alan's walkie-talkie squawked.

"Red team, report! Repeat: red team, report!"

COOKIE HAD BEEN hiding in the lower branches of a beech. From the tree he'd torn a decent-sized stick, not snapping it, but twisting so it came away with a jagged end. Not exactly sharp. But not blunt, either. It was better than nothing.

He'd watched the player and his bodyguard below, waiting for the right moment to strike.

Forget the nervous old guy. He had a beautiful Purdey, but he was shaking like a shitting dog. The bodyguard was dangerous, but the moment Cookie saw him drop his rifle to its strap, he knew the guy was dead meat.

Sure enough, the guard never knew what hit him. Neither of the hunters had bothered looking up, supreme predators that they were, and Cookie dropped silently behind Alan, bare feet on the cool woodland floor. As his left arm encircled Alan's neck, his elbow angled so that his target's carotid artery was fat, his right arm plunged the stick into the exposed flesh.

But the years of drugs and booze and sleeping rough had taken their toll, and even as he let Alan slide to the ground to bleed out in seconds, the old guy was spinning around and leveling his hunting rifle. And where once Cookie's reactions had been as fast as his brain, now the two were out of alignment.

Oakleigh pulled the trigger. Cookie had already seen that he was left-handed and knew how the weapon would pull, and so he twisted in the opposite direction. But even so, he was too slow.

He heard tree bark crack and saw splinters fly a microsecond after he heard the shot. A second later, pain flared along his side and he felt blood pool in the waistband of his jeans.

The stick was still in his hand, so he stepped forward and rammed it into the old guy's throat, cursing him for a coward, as Oakleigh folded to the ground with the stick protruding from his neck.

"Red team, report! Red team, report!" wailed the walkie-talkie. But even though Cookie knew others would be arriving soon, he needed a moment to compose himself, so he leaned against a tree, pressing his palm to the spot where the bullet had grazed him. He pulled up his sweater to inspect the wound. It looked bad, but he knew from painful experience it was nothing to worry about. Blood loss and the fact that he'd be easier to track were the worst of it.

He took stock. The old guy was still twitching. Alan was dead. Cookie reached for the security guard's assault rifle, but when he inspected the grip, he found it inset with some kind of sensor. His heart sank as he tried to operate the safety and found it unresponsive, knowing what the sensor meant: smart-technology. Linked to the user's palm print. And if his guess was correct…

Fuck! The old guy's Purdey was equipped with the same. He tossed it away. From Alan he took a hunting knife. The old guy had a sidearm, also smart-protected and also useless.

The hunting knife would have to do. But now it was time to find out if these Quarry Co. guys were going to fulfil their part of the bargain. He put a hand to his side and started running. Leaves stung his eyes. Twigs lashed him. He stumbled over roots bubbling on the ground and reached to push branches aside as he hurtled forwards in search of sanctuary.

From behind came the crash of gunfire. Overhead, the sound of the drones intensified. They'd spotted him now. The time for stealth was over. He just had to hope he'd given them enough to think about in the meantime, and that the two casualties would slow them down.

Teeth bared, hatred in his bones, he kept running. The trees were thinning. Ahead of him was a peat-covered slope and he hit it fast. Scrambling to the top, he was painfully aware that he'd made himself a visible target, but he was close now. Close to the perimeter.

"If you reach the road you win. The money's yours."

"No matter who I have to kill along the way?"

"Our players expect danger, Mr. Cook. What is the roulette wheel without the risk of losing?"

He'd believed them and, fuck it, why not?

And there it was—the road. It bisected a further stretch of woodland, but this was definitely it. An observation drone buzzed a few feet above him. To his left he heard the sound of approaching engines and saw a Land Rover Defender leaning into the bend, approaching fast. Two men in the front.

They didn't look like they were about to celebrate his victory. He tensed. At his rear the noise of the approaching hunting party was getting louder.

The Defender roared up to his position, passenger door flapping as it drew to a halt. A security guy wielding the same Heckler & Koch assault rifle carried by Alan stepped out and took up position behind the door.

"Where's my money?" called Cookie, with a glance back down into the basin of the wood. He could see the blurry outlines of players and their security among the trees, the crackle of comms. "You said if I reached the road I win," he pressed.

Ignoring him, the passenger had braced his rifle on the sill of his window and was speaking into a walkie-talkie, saying something Cookie couldn't hear. Receiving orders.

"Come on, you bastards. I reached the fucking road, now where's my money?"

The passenger had finished on the walkie-talkie, and Cookie had been shot at enough times to know the signs of it happening again. There was no prize money. No winning. No survival. There were just hunters and prey. Just an old fool and a man about to gun him down.

The passenger squeezed off bullets that zinged over Cookie's head as he tucked in and let himself roll back to the bottom of the slope.

I can do this, he thought. He'd fought in Afghanistan. He'd fought with the best, against the best. He could go up against a bunch of rich geriatric thrill-seekers and come out on top—security or no security. *Yes.* He was going to get out of this and then he was going to make the fuckers pay.

He could do it. Who dares wins.

Then a bullet ripped the top of Cookie's head off—a bullet fired from a TrackingPoint precision-guided bolt-action rifle.

"Oh, good shot, Mr. Miyake," said the players as they emerged from the undergrowth in order to survey the kill.

They were already looking forward to the post-hunt meal.

ABOUT THE AUTHORS

JAMES PATTERSON has written more bestsellers and created more enduring fictional characters than any other novelist writing today. He lives in Florida with his family.

Since the debut of his first novel, *The Narrowback*, **MICHAEL LEDWIDGE** has written fourteen additional novels, a dozen of them *New York Times* bestsellers coauthored with James Patterson.

"ALEX CROSS, I'M COMING FOR YOU...."

Gary Soneji, the killer from *Along Came a Spider,* has been dead for more than ten years—but Cross swears he saw Soneji gun down his partner. Is Cross's worst enemy back from the grave?

Nothing will prepare you for the wicked truth.

Read the next riveting, pulse-racing Alex Cross adventure, available now only from

BOOKSHOTS

"I'M NOT ON TRIAL. SAN FRANCISCO IS."

Drug cartel boss the Kingfisher has a reputation for being violent and merciless. And after he's finally caught, he's set to stand trial for his vicious crimes—until he begins unleashing chaos and terror upon the lawyers, jurors, and police associated with the case. The city is paralyzed, and Detective Lindsay Boxer is caught in the eye of the storm.

Will the Women's Murder Club make it out alive—or will a sudden courtroom snare ensure their last breaths?

Read the new Women's Murder Club story, available now only from

BOOK**SHOTS**

CAN A LITTLE BLACK DRESS CHANGE EVERYTHING?

Divorced magazine editor Jane Avery is content with spending her nights alone—until she finds *The Dress*. Suddenly she's surrendering to dark desires, and New York City has become her erotic playground. But what begins as a sultry fantasy has gone too far....

And her next conquest could be her last.

Check out the steamy cliffhanger *Little Black Dress*, available now from

BOOK**SHOTS**

Looking to Fall in Love in Just One Night?
Introducing BookShots Flames:

original romances presented by James Patterson that fit into your busy life.

Featuring Love Stories by:

New York Times bestselling author Jen McLaughlin

New York Times bestselling author Samantha Towle

USA Today bestselling author Erin Knightley

Elizabeth Hayley

Jessica Linden

Codi Gary

Laurie Horowitz

…and many others!

Available only from

James Patterson's
BOOKSHOTS
Flames

SHE NEVER EXPECTED TO FALL IN LOVE WITH A COWBOY....

Rodeo king Tanner Callen isn't looking to be tied down anytime soon. When he sees Madeline Harper at a local honky-tonk—even though everything about her screams New York City—he brings out every trick in his playbook to take her home.

But soon he learns that he doesn't just want her for a night.

Instead, he hopes for forever.

Read the heartwarming new romance, *Learning to Ride*, available now from